THE
BEST TREASURY
OF STORIES
for Children

BCA

LONDON   NEW YORK   SYDNEY   TORONTO

First published in Great Britain in 1995 by Hodder Children's Books

This edition published 1996 by BCA
by arrangement with Hodder Children's Books

CN 4683

Typeset by Avon Dataset Ltd, Bidford-on-Avon, Warks
Printed and bound in Great Britain by
Mackays of Chatham plc, Chatham, Kent

Contents

Petticoat Palm

Joan Aiken

Petticoat Palm

Joan Aiken

When Joe went to stay with Grandma Quex the sea amazed him. For where Joe lived, the sea was grey and flat, and it lay dull and sad, on the other side of a grey, flat, stony beach.

But where Grandma Quex lived the sea was blue and clear, the colour of ink, and it roared and thrashed, in sheets of white foam, at the foot of a green grassy and black rocky cliff.

Grandma's palm tree stood on the top of the cliff and waved its fan-shaped branches wildly, as if it were sending messages to the tossing sea.

"Of course I have to take great care of it," said Grandma. "It is *much* too far north for a palm tree to be growing. But your grandfather planted it and I'd hate to lose it."

A date in her diary every six months was ringed with red ink and the letters DOT.

"That stands for Department of Trees," said Grandma. "They think my palm tree is so important that they send a man every six months to make sure I am looking after it properly."

Joe didn't see how you could look after a palm tree. But one morning the radio weather forecast said, "There will be severe ground frost tonight in northern counties, even in coastal areas. And the wind chill factor will make it even colder."

"My gracious," said Grandma Quex. "And it's this evening that the DOT man makes his call. You'll have to help me, Joe. We must wrap up the tree."

Grandma Quex had a big old stone house, which stood sheltered in a dent of the cliff. The top floor of the house was all huge attics, which held junk and treasures and mysteries from past times, going back hundreds of years.

"These things will do to wrap up the palm tree," said Grandma, opening trunks in one of the attics. And she pulled out petticoats and pantalettes and a huge quilted crinoline, as big as an air balloon. And she pulled out shawls and chemises and shirts, she pulled out vests and waistcoats and wigs and wrappers.

"Fetch out the kitchen steps, Joe," she said, "and we'll do this job properly."

Grishkin, Grandma's cat, sat watching them all through the afternoon as they wrapped and dressed the palm tree. He thought they had gone mad.

By the end of the afternoon there was not a single inch of the tree to be seen. They had wrapped up its furry, webby trunk in petticoats and crinolines. They had pinned shawls and wimples and yashmaks and cloaks and plaids and mantles over its fan-shaped branches.

Joe thought the tree looked terrific.

"If only it could dance," he said.

"Now the DOT man can come just as soon as he likes," said Grandma. "But I'm worn out. I'm going in to make a cup of tea."

The Evening Star came out while Joe was standing on the cliff, admiring Grandma's palm tree in its fancy dress.

"Star light, star bright," said Joe, "first star I see tonight, I wish I may, I wish I might, have the wish I wish tonight. I wish that palm tree could dance."

No sooner were the words out of Joe's mouth then off danced the tree, tweaking itself out of the ground and capering down the steep hill as if it were happy to be set free at last!

"Hey!" bawled Joe. "Hey! Come back! You can't go off like that!"

But the tree paid no attention. Where it had stood was a deep hole, and something flashed at the bottom. Joe reached down and grabbed whatever it was, then he set off at top speed after the palm tree.

He was panting and gulping and horrified.

Somehow the palm tree had to be stopped, had to be brought back and set in its place, before Grandma came out and saw what had happened, before the DOT man came on his visit of inspection. Or he might say that Grandma was not fit to be in charge of a palm tree.

The palm tree went dancing and skipping down the cliff path. It seemed quite drunk with joy. It bounced, it whirled, it leaned from side to side.

"One thing," thought Joe, "we tied those clothes on really tight, Grandma and I. At least they aren't coming off."

Joe had a piece of chalk in his pocket. He drew arrows on the path, in case Grandma came out, to show where they had gone.

Luckily at the foot of the cliff path there was a big puddle of water, where the waves had splashed over.

The palm tree stopped to admire its reflection, and Joe was able to catch up.

"Please, tree, go back where you belong!"

But the tree danced on down the path.

Now they came to a kissing-gate, a wishing-gate, which was the entrance to the cliff path. The gate was like a stubby wooden cross, set

on top of a post, and you pushed it round in order to go through. The palm tree edged its wrapped-up shape past the first arm of the kissing gate.

And Joe cried out:

> "Gate, gate, wishing-gate
> Grant my wish, please don't wait
> Please, please co-operate
> Save my Grandma from disgrace
> Put the palm tree in its place!"

The palm tree cocked its branches to one side as if it was listening. Then it spun through the kissing-gate – all the way round – and went dancing back up the path, as fast as it had danced down.

Joe went panting after, rubbing out the chalk arrows as he went.

And when he got back to Grandma's house, he saw the palm tree jump into its hole and settle down with a shrug and a wriggle and a twitch.

Oh well! it seemed to be saying. I had a run. And I did have fun.

And it slipped in not a moment too soon, for there was the DOT man, coming up the road in his red car, and here was Grandma coming out of the old stone house.

"Well, sir!" she said proudly. "We've got our tree nicely wrapped up, as you can see!"

"You have indeed!" said the tree man. And he walked round the tree, admiring it.

Joe had a moment's horrible fright. Where was the cat, Grishkin? Could he possibly have been down in the hole, sniffing about, when the palm tree hopped back into place?

But then, with a huge gulp of relief, Joe saw Grishkin rubbing in a friendly way against the garden gate-post.

"No," said the tree man, walking round yet again. "The way you've got that tree snugged up, I reckon it should be good for another hundred years. And I'd not say no to a cup of tea, Mrs Quex!"

They all went inside for a cup of tea. And Joe pulled out the shiny thing he had put in his pocket.

"Why!" said Grandma. "Where in the world did you pick that up? Your grandfather's watch, that's been lost since I was a young girl . . . ?"

La Belle Lulu Labelle

Karen Wallace

La Belle Lulu Labelle

Karen Wallace

Once there was a little girl called La Belle Lulu Labelle. She lived with her mother and father and a big white poodle called Patrick.

Lulu had thick black hair and eyes as brown as chestnuts. Her mother would look at her and sigh. She sighed because Lulu never brushed her hair, hardly ever changed her clothes and never ever wore a dress. Lulu wasn't interested in things like that. She only wanted to be with Patrick.

Every day Lulu made Patrick a new clip-on bow tie for his collar.

Every day Patrick walked with Lulu to school. When she went swimming, he watched from the gallery. When she did her homework, he lay under her desk and kept her feet warm.

One evening Lulu came down to supper. Her shirt was ripped and muddy. Her hair looked like a bird's nest. On the table was a snowy cauliflower in cream sauce with buttered peas and fresh green beans.

Lulu sat down. "I hate vegetables," she said. "Patrick doesn't eat vegetables. Why should I?"

"Ooh, la, la, Lulu!" cried Mrs Labelle, rolling her eyes and wringing her hands. "Whatever next?"

Her father twitched his moustache. "Patrick is a dog," he said. "Dogs don't eat vegetables."

Lulu pointed her chin at the ceiling. "Then nor shall I," she declared. "I shall eat only bread and cheese."

So the next day Lulu ate bread and cheese for breakfast, a cheese sandwich for lunch and cheese on toast for supper.

It was the same the next day and the day after that.

It was the same the next week and the week after that.

"Don't you get fed up with bread and cheese?" asked her friend, Jeanette.

"No," said Lulu. "I like it." She smiled and Jeanette noticed something rather strange.

Lulu's front teeth seemed to have grown and her ears were strangely furry.

That night Lulu didn't sleep in her bed. She decided she didn't like her pretty patchwork quilt.

Instead she curled up inside a large pile of leaves she had hidden in her cupboard.

The next morning Lulu had a piano lesson. As she sat down on her stool, the teacher's eyes popped out of his head. A grey tail was hanging from the hem of Lulu's skirt! As she played, it twitched in time to the music.

That afternoon Lulu had an art lesson and she painted a picture of herself.

When the teacher saw it, she jumped onto a chair and screamed.

It was a picture of a mouse.

"I'm sorry to inform you that your daughter has turned into a mouse," said the headmaster.

"What shall we do?" cried Mrs Labelle.

"Take her to the vet," said the headmaster.

"No child of mine goes to a vet!" shouted Mr Labelle. "She might catch fleas in the waiting room. I shall take her to a doctor immediately."

The doctor examined Lulu.

He counted her whiskers.

He measured the length of her tail.

He shone a little torch in her furry ears and felt the sharpness of her long front teeth.

"She is definitely a mouse," he said.

"Ooh, la, la!" cried Mrs Labelle, rolling her eyes and wringing her hands. "What can we do?"

"She must have no more cheese," said the doctor sternly. "She must eat only vegetables."

"But I like being a mouse," said Lulu. "I always win at hide and seek and if I don't like my lessons, I squeeze underneath the floorboards." She pulled a piece of cheese from her pocket and nibbled it.

Then she scampered from the room.

It didn't matter what kind of vegetables Mrs Labelle cooked. It didn't matter whether they were raw, fried, steamed or roasted.

Lulu would not touch them.

After a while, Mrs Labelle gave up. She got used to sweeping the leaves from her daughter's cupboard instead of making her bed.

She even cut little holes in Lulu's trousers so her tail would be more comfortable.

Mr Labelle gave up, too. He used to read Lulu fairy tales. But she didn't like them any more. None of the princes and princesses were mice.

So he read her mouse adventure stories and changed the endings so the mice always won.

As for Patrick, he spent his time lying alone outside the back door.

Lulu didn't make him bow ties any more.

He never went to school with her. And when she was at home she was too busy making nests in the sofa or looking for crumbs on the kitchen floor to play with him.

She even stopped swimming.

"Mice don't swim," said Lulu, firmly.

One day, Lulu was lying in the garden chewing

apple pips and admiring her tiny curled nails.

She didn't take much notice when the cat next door sat down beside her.

Then he moved closer. Suddenly she could smell his hot fishy breath.

Lulu's mouse heart went Pop! in her chest.

THAT CAT WANTS TO EAT ME! she thought to herself.

As fast as she could she ran across the garden.

The cat ran after her.

"Help! Help!" shouted Lulu. But because she was only a mouse, her shout was barely a squeak.

The cat was just behind her when she stumbled in the grass. "Someone help me!" she sobbed as she hit the ground with the tiniest of thuds.

Outside the back door, Patrick pricked up his ears and bounded across the garden.

Just as the cat opened his mouth to gobble Lulu up, Patrick jumped on top of him!

Lulu lay on the ground and howled. "I don't want to be a mouse any more," she cried. "I want to be a girl again." Patrick howled, too. He was unhappy because she was unhappy.

Mrs Labelle ran out from the kitchen. She

picked up her tiny daughter and kissed her furry pink ears.

"Ooh, la, la, Lulu," she said, gently. "Don't cry."

The doctor was right.

After a week or two of eating only vegetables, Lulu changed back into a little girl.

On the evening the doctor pronounced her completely better, Lulu came down to supper. She was wearing a brand new dress and her hair was tied up with a green ribbon.

"Ooh, la, la, Lulu!" cried Mrs Labelle, clapping her hands. "How lovely you look!"

On the table was a snowy cauliflower in a cream sauce with buttered peas and fresh green beans.

Lulu sat down. "I love vegetables," she cried, helping herself to a big plateful of everything.

"And what about Patrick?" asked her father with a twinkle in his eye. "Does *he* like vegetables?"

"He loves vegetables, too," replied Lulu Labelle, grinning.

And sure enough, there was Patrick, lying under the table and chewing on a carrot.

The Trouble with Anteaters

David Sutherland

The Trouble with Anteaters

David Sutherland

Max had an anteater but he soon found that it ate other things as well. One day it ate his mum's earrings. It wouldn't have been so bad if she hadn't been wearing them at the time. She was fairly upset.

The anteater was called Lenny and Max loved him terribly. They did lots of things together, like going for bicycle rides, playing frisbee in the park or going to the cinema. Some days they went to visit Max's Uncle Harold. Other days they went to the zoo to visit Lenny's cousins.

27

The only thing Max didn't like was when Lenny kissed him.

Anteaters, as you may know, kiss in the same way as dogs, only more so. Their tongues are not only *very* long, but also *very* sticky and slobbery. Of course, Lenny didn't understand that people don't normally like being kissed by a giant, hairy, Venezuelan anteater; he just happened to be very affectionate.

He liked to give Max a big kiss every day when he got home from school. He kissed Max's dad when he came home from work. He kissed Max's mum usually when she least expected it. (You must remember that an anteater can kiss from more than five feet away – even around corners!)

Max's dad got especially cross at times. He didn't like being covered in anteater slobber after a hard day at work. "Lenny, you horrible beast!" he'd shout. "Do that again and I'll cut your tongue off!" But of course he never did.

When it was Pet Day at Max's school, all the other kids came with their cats and dogs and hamsters, but he was the only one with a giant, hairy, Venezuelan anteater. Max brushed his black and white coat until it shone. "Please try to behave yourself for once," Max asked him.

"And don't go kissing Miss Dorrington or you'll be sent home!"

Everything would have been fine if Julia Fitzsimmons hadn't brought her Ant Farm.

An Ant Farm is essentially a bit of earth stuck between two pieces of glass with ants in it. You watch them walking around in their tunnels underground and it can be quite interesting – that is, if you like ants.

Well, it just so happened there was someone present who liked ants very much.

Everyone sat in a circle with their pets. Julia Fitzsimmons was directly across from Max. Lenny couldn't take his eyes off the Ant Farm.

Suddenly, without warning, he shot out his tongue! *SPLATT!* He hit the glass from across the room. Again and again he tried, but he didn't get a single ant and he couldn't understand why. Everyone laughed and Lenny looked very confused and disappointed. "Lenny's stupid," said Julia Fitzsimmons. "Doesn't he realise that he can't eat the ants through the glass?"

Everyone laughed again. Everyone except Max. He knew Lenny wasn't stupid at all. "He's probably a lot smarter than you'll ever be, Julia Fitzsimmons," he whispered to himself.

No sooner had he said this than Lenny

wriggled out of his arms and pounced across the room. Thinking she was going to be attacked, Julia Fitzsimmons shrieked and jumped back. But Lenny wasn't interested in her.

He knocked over the Ant Farm with his front paws. The glass smashed to bits and suddenly there were hundreds of ants everywhere! What a treat! Lenny lapped them up greedily with his long sticky tongue.

"Stop him! Stop him!" shouted Julia Fitzsimmons hysterically. "He's eating all my lovely pet ants!"

By the time Max could pull him away, there were hardly any ants left. Poor Julia was in tears. "Max," cried Miss Dorrington, "I think perhaps you ought to take Lenny home. He's done quite enough damage for one day!"

As soon as Lenny heard Miss Dorrington say his name, he simply had to give her a big sloppy kiss. He kissed Julia Fitzsimmons too, to thank her for the nice lunch, even though she had called him stupid. He was very happy.

Max was not very happy. On the way home, he told Lenny off. "Why are you so naughty all the time? You'll never win the 'Best Behaved Pet' award like that you know!"

But that afternoon things went from bad to

worse. The vicar had come to have tea with Max's mum. They sat on the sofa in the living room, talking about the church fête the following week. Max got on with his homework. Lenny was asleep on the carpet.

Max was vaguely aware of the sound of a fly buzzing around the room, but he took no notice. The vicar, a kindly man called Wilfred Dribble, was busy talking to Max's mum and he took no notice either – even when the fly landed on his nose.

But Lenny heard the buzzing, even in his sleep. He opened one eye and spotted the fly straight away. Without even raising his head, he shot his tongue out across the room. *SPLATT!* A bullseye! Poor Vicar Dribble didn't know what had hit him! He shrieked and flung his tea cup into the air and Max's mum had to jump to avoid getting scalded! Accidently she knocked over a lamp, which smashed down on the mantelpiece, sending two glass vases and an antique clock crashing to the floor!

Lenny calmly swallowed the fly and licked his lips as if nothing had happened. Max covered his eyes in despair, peering out at the wreckage between two fingers.

"Lenny!" his mum screamed. "Out of this house right now! OUT!"

Poor Lenny slunk away, not even realising what he'd done wrong. Max put him out in the garden.

"Lenny," he said, "that's the second disaster you've caused today! First you ate all Julia Fitzsimmons' ants and just now you nearly gave the vicar a heart attack! You can't go eating flies off people's noses like that. It's not polite. You're a bad anteater!"

Lenny looked up guiltily and gave Max a big slobbery kiss. "*YUCK!*" cried Max, wiping his face on his sleeve. "And stop kissing everyone all the time! If you don't stop misbehaving, Dad will sell you to the zoo!" Lenny looked at Max with his tiny black eyes and turned his head to one side. Then he scampered off and zapped a big ant on the garden wall.

When Max's dad came home that evening, he heard all about the disaster in the sitting room and he was not best pleased. "Max," he said sternly, "this has gone on long enough. Anteaters simply do not make very good house pets. Lenny has got to go."

This was the worst possible news. Lenny was his best friend in the world! Max knew his father was right, but it made him terribly depressed. He couldn't imagine visiting poor

Lenny at the zoo! He thought of him living in a cage, being stared at day after day by a lot of dumb tourists. It was unbearable!

That evening Max couldn't get to sleep. He lay awake for hours thinking about everything that had happened. Looking out of the window, he could see Lenny lying fast asleep in the garden.

"Sweet dreams, Lenny," Max whispered. "Who knows where you'll be this time tomorrow . . ."

He lay in bed with his eyes open, staring at the ceiling. It was very late. The house was dark and silent. His parents were fast asleep. Only Max was awake; awake and thirsty. Finally he got up and went down to the kitchen to get a drink.

The stairs creaked. Max's shadow crept along the wall beside him. He always found it exciting and a little bit scary going downstairs at night when everyone else was asleep, but he made it to the kitchen and got a drink of water without even turning on the light.

Putting away the glass, he turned around. He took one step, then suddenly – he bumped straight into a strange man with a mask! There was a burglar in the house!

They both jumped back. It was impossible to

say who was more startled! Max screamed and the burglar dashed past him, out of the kitchen door and into the garden. By this time, Max's parents were awake and rushing down the stairs to see what all the noise was about.

Max ran to the kitchen window and shouted, "Lenny! Get him Lenny! Don't let him get away!"

The burglar sprinted across the garden, preparing for a great leap over the back wall. But just as he jumped – *ZAPP!* Lenny's laser-quick tongue shot out and caught him by one leg! The burglar crashed to the ground and Lenny sat on his head so he couldn't move until the police came.

The police sergeant was very impressed. "That there beast deserves a medal if you ask me," he said. Lenny completely agreed and gave the policeman a big sloppy anteater kiss to say so.

Max's dad was pretty impressed too. "You won't sell him to the zoo now, will you Dad?" Max asked hopefully. "Lenny can stay now, can't he?"

"Oh, I guess so. But just make sure he behaves himself!"

"Did you hear that, Lenny?" Max asked. "You can stay! But you've got to be good! Understand?"

Unfortunately, Lenny didn't understand a thing. But everyone seemed to be pleased and that made him happy. So he gave Max's dad an enormously slobbery goodnight kiss and scampered up the stairs. He curled up on Max's bed and instantly fell fast asleep, dreaming about . . . What do you think? Ants, I suppose!

Queen Isabel

Joyce Dunbar

Queen Isabel

Joyce Dunbar

Let me tell you about Isabel. She might have seemed like an ordinary little girl but Isabel had a secret.

Really, she was a QUEEN!

How did she know she was a queen?

After all, she had no crown, only a squashed sun hat and a woolly bobble hat and a hood on her cagoule.

She had no throne to sit on, only a bean-bag chair to call her own.

She had no palace and no servants, only an

ordinary house with an ordinary mother and father. She had no one to rule over, except a baby brother called Timmy and a cat, and they didn't count because they wouldn't do as she said.

She didn't even have a Kingdom, just a long thin garden with a cherry tree that never grew any cherries.

But still, she knew she was a queen.

It was a feeling, deep inside her, that somehow she was special, that she was the *middle of the world*.

"When did the world begin?" she asked her mother.

"Oh, millions and millions of years ago, before you were born."

"What was it like?" asked Isabel.

"I don't really know," said her mother. "There were dinosaurs and—"

"Did you like the dinosaurs?" asked Isabel.

"I don't know," said her mother. "I wasn't around to see them."

"When will the world end?" asked Isabel.

"Not for ages and ages," said her mother. "Not for millions and millions of years. Now I must go and give Timmy his bath."

So Isabel talked to Ted.

"When I am queen, we can do as we want.

We won't let the world end, will we Ted? Not ever, ever, ever!"

Isabel practised being a queen. She put on her cloak, which was a curtain of shiny brocade, and made herself a paper crown. She tried to teach Ted to walk backwards.

"That's what you do with queens, Ted. When you leave the room, you mustn't take your eyes off a queen."

But Ted couldn't walk backwards. He couldn't walk at all but just kept falling over.

"Ah, but when I am queen, Ted, you'll be able to walk and *talk* as well – and *I* shall be able to *fly*!"

Isabel knew the day would come when it would all be for real. The curtain would rise, the bells would ring and the announcement would be made:

"All hail Queen Isabel! Long live Queen Isabel."

And she would order a banquet, and a fireworks display, and cherries on the cherry tree in the garden. She couldn't wait for that special day! She hoped it would come very soon.

It did.

"It's a very special day for you soon, isn't it my girl," said her father one supper-time.

"Is it?" said Isabel.

"Yes," said her father. "Our little Isabel will be starting school! Look what I've got for you!"

He showed her a brightly coloured rucksack and a new packet of felt-tip pens and a pencil with a frog rubber on the end. Her mother gave her a lunch box. Isabel was kitted out with a new skirt and jumper, socks, shoes and shorts and pumps. Then her mother took her to see her new school which was a long way away, in the town.

"It's very big isn't it?" said Isabel, staring through the huge iron gates. "Will I get lost?"

"There'll be plenty of people to look after you," said her mother, "and look, there's a climbing frame for you to play on and a bell up there in the bell tower."

And Isabel knew. She knew that the school was really a palace. She knew that the rucksack would become a golden coach and the pencil with the frog rubber was a royal sceptre, and that soon she would be crowned.

The night before school she hardly slept at all. Her stomach was so full of butterflies! "I'm glad you're coming with me," she said to Ted. "I hope I'll be a good sort of queen."

Her mother watched from the school gates and left her to play in the playground. There were so many other children! Isabel didn't know a single one. Then the bell rang.

Bing-bong-boiiing.

The children rushed to stand in line. A bunch of them were pushing and shoving to stand in front.

"*I* should stand in front," Isabel explained.

"No, *I* should!" said a much bigger girl with ginger hair.

"Never mind," Isabel whispered to Ted. "This is all part of the act. It's just to try me out."

Then they followed the teacher into a big hall. The moment had come! There was a stage, and a crowd of chattering children.

"Shhhhhh! Children! Shhhhhhh!" said the lady at the front.

Slowly, slowly, the noise died down. Slowly the children settled.

"Good morning children," said the lady at the front.

"Good morning Mrs Brown," chanted the children.

"Now, I want you to listen very carefully – ' she began. "I have something important to tell you."

Isabel closed her eyes and held on to Ted. She felt dizzy. She didn't want to be a queen! She wouldn't know what to do! She wanted to go to the loo and didn't even know where the cloakrooms were! "Please, oh please, not yet," she whispered.

This time she was lucky. The lady at the front didn't say anything at all about queens. Instead she talked about the school and the playtimes and the lovely day they were going to have. Then a piano began to play and everyone sang a song. But it wasn't a royal anthem. It was a song about a blackbird that spoke. Isabel breathed a sigh of relief. She didn't have to be a queen just yet.

The teacher took them to the cloakroom. "And you're Isabel aren't you?" she said. "Look, this is your coat peg with your name on it."

Isabel handed her coat to the teacher to hang up, just like her mother did at home. She wondered if the teacher would curtsey.

She didn't. "Oh no, Isabel," she said. "You hang your coat up yourself. And see, there are the toilets. Remember to wash your hands."

In the classroom Isabel was shown to a table which she shared with several other children. They didn't curtsey either; they took no notice of her at all. So Isabel took out her pencil with the frog rubber and her new packet of felt tips and she drew a picture of a queen . . .

. . . before she knew where she was, the bell was ringing again.

Bing-bong-boiiing.

The other children raced for the door. Only Isabel stayed where she was.

"Come back this minute!" said the teacher. "That is *not* the proper way to leave the room!"

Isabel knew what was going to happen. She had told Ted all about the proper way. The children would be made to walk backwards because they shouldn't take their eyes off a queen. But oh dear, no! She didn't want to be a queen just yet. "Please, oh please, not now," she murmured.

And once again she was spared. The teacher kept her secret! The children had to sit quietly and leave one at a time, then Isabel left too. It was all part of the act.

The day was full of hustle and bustle. There was a *bing-bong-boiiing* at mid-day and yet again no announcement was made. They all had lunch in the dining room. There was a *bing-bong-boiiing* in the afternoon and they all had a second playtime. In between they did all sorts of things. They played with the sand tray and in the wendy house and they made plasticine models. They painted and cut things out and stuck them down.

Yet Isabel was puzzled. If it was all part of an act, the other children played it very well – just as if it were real. They wouldn't even do as she said:

"I'll do the cooking," she announced in the wendy house.

"No, I'll do the cooking!" said a boy with rosy cheeks, snatching the saucepan off her.

Indeed, as the day wore on, Isabel began to wonder if she really wanted to be a queen. She sat in the book corner with Ted and had a word with him about it.

"You see Ted, I'll have to know where everything is, and the words of the songs, and what to order for lunch. And you see Ted, I can't even *read*. I'm sure that queens can read. Do you think I could change my mind and not be a queen after all?"

It was three o'clock. Isabel was tired. The other children were tired.

"Now children," said the teacher. "I want you all to put your things away on the shelves. You can see where they go. And then I want you to come and sit by me on the mat. This is a very special part of the day."

Isabel's heart beat faster. She held on to Ted. The teacher sat on a chair and all the children sat round her.

"Shhhhhh! Shhhhh! Shhhhhhh!" said the teacher. "Sit still, settle down, and be as quiet as you can. Then *listen*."

Some children still shuffled and whispered, but soon all was quiet. Isabel closed her eyes. The dreadful moment had come. All of the children would know. The world was a very big place and she was much too small to be a queen. She couldn't bear it for one moment longer. She jumped up, with Ted in her arms.

"*I don't want to be a queen!*" she wailed, and burst into floods of tears.

47

"Isabel! What's the matter?" asked the teacher, scooping her up onto her lap.

"I don't want to be a queen," sobbed Isabel. "I don't think I'm special after all."

"Of course you're special," said the teacher. "You're *all* special. But you can be especially special today Isabel and sit on my lap while I read a story to everyone."

And Isabel did.

And how special Isabel felt! And how she loved the story, about Barbar, the elephant, who wore a crown.

As the teacher reached the end of the story, the bell rang for the last time that day.

Bing-bong-boiiing. It was hometime.

That night Isabel had a long talk with Ted. "You don't have to walk backwards Ted, *never never never*, because I don't want to be a queen *ever, ever, ever*. I like being a little girl. There's only one thing Ted – the cherry tree in the garden. Now it won't ever grow any cherries."

But do you know, the very next year – it did!

Grandpa Fogarty and the Tangerine Shell

Geoffrey Patterson

Grandpa Fogarty and the Tangerine Shell

Geoffrey Patterson

"Do you believe in magic, Grandpa Fogarty?" asked Luke.

Grandpa Fogarty didn't answer, but stared out of the window at the sea.

Grandpa Fogarty had once been a sailor, but that was long ago. Nowadays, he spent most of the day combing the shore, peering through his pebble glasses at anything the tide might wash up onto the beach – usually shells that he would hold to his ear or, sometimes, driftwood that reminded him of some bird or

53

strange animal he'd once seen on his travels.

Grandpa Fogarty lived alone with his dog, Pip, except for a few weeks in the summer when Luke came to stay.

"Grandpa," Luke tried again. "Grandpa, do you believe in ghosts and things that go bump in the night?"

Silence.

"Grandpa Fogarty!" cried Luke, getting cross. "I'm asking you something!"

But Grandpa Fogarty ignored Luke's question and kept on staring out of the window.

"Please, Grandpa, do you believe in tiny voices that . . ?"

Grandpa Fogarty swung round. "No, I don't, you silly boy! What a load of rubbish! Tiny voices, indeed!" And with that, he stomped out of the kitchen into the garden.

Grandpa Fogarty was in a very bad mood, and Luke knew why. He had lost his Special Tin Box – the box that held all his most precious treasures: his brass compass, the penknife with the bone handle, the gold coin he had found on the beach, and the watch that chimed on a silvery chain. For one long year, Grandpa Fogarty had planned to give the Special Tin Box to Luke on the first day of his holiday. It was now three days since Luke had arrived and Grandpa Fogarty still couldn't remember where he had tucked it.

"We'd better see what *we* can do," said Luke to Pip. So, while Grandpa Fogarty was in the garden, they hunted high and low . . . on top of the chest, under the table, inside the cupboard, between the books . . . And, wonder of wonders, they did at last come upon it – behind the clock!

Luke and Pip rushed into the garden to tell Grandpa Fogarty the good news, but they caught him on the hop.

"Out of my way, you two!"

"Grandpa, you'll never guess!"

"Hang on, boy," said Grandpa Fogarty, "I've got to go in. I must catch the Weather Forecast!" And he pushed past Luke and went into the kitchen to switch on the radio.

"But Grandpa!, it's the —"

"You're not *still* going on about magic and tiny voices, are you?" bellowed Grandpa Fogarty. "Out of my way now, and *after* the Weather Forecast we'll go for a good, long walk!"

But Luke had a plan. There were over one hundred shells on the mantelpiece and he popped one of them into his pocket before tiptoeing out of the door. Outside, beyond the garden gate, there was a rock pointing like a finger into the sky. Luke put the shell – it was the colour of a tangerine – on top of the rock where Grandpa couldn't fail to spot it. Then he and the dog tucked themselves well out of sight behind the rock.

A moment or two later, Grandpa Fogarty stomped down the path, through the gate, and on to the beach, in search of Luke and Pip. Almost immediately, the tangerine-coloured shell caught his eye.

"Well, I never!" he said. "*That*'s a beauty!" And he held it gently to his ear ...

And the shell SAID something! It SPOKE to him in a little, tiny voice.

56

"Bless my soul!" roared Grandpa Fogarty. "I must be going crackers!" But he held the shell to his ear again.

And the tiny voice was still speaking: "Look behind the clock!" It whispered – "Behind the clock . . . the clock . . ."

"I *am* crackers!" muttered Grandpa Fogarty, but he pocketed the shell and stumbled back through the gate, up the path and into the house. And there it was – his Special Tin Box – behind the clock, just where he'd left it!

"Hooray!" cried Grandpa Fogarty, "I've found the Special Tin Box! Come and get your Special Tin Box, Luke!" Luke and Pip scampered gleefully into the house.

Grandpa Fogarty gave his grandson a big hug and threw the dog a bone to celebrate! "I hope you'll both forgive me for being so grumpy this morning. I thought I'd lost it for ever!" So saying, he handed the Special Tin Box over to Luke.

"Of course we will!" said Luke, sneaking a look at all the familiar treasures. "And thank you, Grandpa Fogarty, very much."

An hour or two later, Luke and Pip and Grandpa Fogarty were sitting cosily by the fire, enjoying their cocoa and biscuits.

"Grandpa, I must ask you something," said Luke. "*Do* you believe in magic and ghosts and things that go bump in the night . . . and tiny voices and things like that?"

Then Grandpa Fogarty, smiling broadly, gave Luke the answer he had been waiting for all day.

"Yes, Luke, I think I *do*. I do believe I do!"

Boris the Birthday Bear

Jenny Alexander

Boris the Birthday Bear

Jenny Alexander

"It's no good!" said Boris. "I'm not coming out!"
Benjamin peered into the darkness under the
bed, where the old bear was hiding.

"Come on, Boris," he said. "You can't stay
there all day. You'll miss your party."

"That's why I'm hiding," said Boris. "I hate
parties!"

It was Boris's birthday. He was seven, which
is quite old for a teddy. He had lost half
an eye, and most of his fur. One of his ears
was a bit chewed, and one of his paws was

crooked. But Benjamin loved him.

"What do you mean, you hate parties?" Benjamin asked. "Parties are great fun!"

"I'm sure they are – if you happen to like lying face down in a bowl of jelly for two hours . . ."

They both remembered Boris's second birthday.

"That was ages ago," Benjamin said, at last. "All your other parties have been fun."

"Oh, yes!" Boris agreed. "If you happen to like having your arm ripped off in a game of Ring o' Roses."

They both remembered his third birthday. Benjamin frowned. It looked as if Boris was going to have one of his grumpy days.

"All right, then," he said. "So we've had a few accidents. But last year's party was fun, wasn't it?"

"Great fun," said Boris, "if you happen to like setting fire to your nose!"

"Oh, yes," said Benjamin, remembering. "Well, I'll blow your candles out for you this time, OK?"

He reached under the bed, but his arm wasn't quite long enough. The tips of his fingers touched Boris's leg, but he couldn't grab hold of it.

"It's no good!" said Boris. "I'm not coming out!"

"Have you found him, yet?" Sarah asked, putting her head round the door.

Sarah was Benjamin's sister. She was twelve years old, and nearly grown up. She peered under the bed, too.

"Doesn't he want to come out?" she said.

She knelt down beside Benjamin and reached under the bed. Her arm was much longer than his.

"Come on, Birthday Boy," she said, grabbing hold of Boris, and pulling him out.

Boris gave her one of his fiercest looks.

"It's no good looking at me like that," she told him. "It's your birthday, and you've jolly well got to enjoy it!"

"Yes," added Benjamin. "And besides, Mum's already made the cake."

Every year, Mum made a teddy-shaped cake for Boris. It was dark chocolate brown, like he used to be, before his fur fell out. It had a red cherry nose, and two brown chocolate-button eyes, not broken.

"It's Boris in his young days," she said. "I'm afraid I can't do grey icing!"

"Who shall we invite to his party?" Benjamin asked.

"No-one," said Mum. "He's too old for a party."

"Thank goodness someone around here has some sense!" thought Boris.

But Benjamin was very sad.

"I know what!" said Sarah. "He could have a trip instead. Trips are great fun!"

Boris groaned.

"I'm sure they are," he said, "if you happen to like having your ear chewed off by a hungry raccoon!"

"That was your own fault," Benjamin said, "for jumping out of my back-pack. And anyway, it doesn't have to be the zoo."

"How about the fair?" said Sarah. "That's great fun, too."

"I'm sure it is," said Boris, "if you happen to like being dropped from the top of the big wheel, and having your eye broken in half!"

"That was your own fault, too," Benjamin told him. "You shouldn't have been leaning out."

"The play park, then," said Sarah. "You can't get safer than that."

"Oh, yes," said Boris. "That's great fun, if you happen to like having all your fur rubbed off, going down the slide!"

Mum laughed.

"Oh, my! Isn't he grumpy today?" she said.

"But never mind – we can't have a trip anyway, because it's raining."

"Thank goodness someone around here has some sense!" thought Boris.

"But we could go for a swim!" Sarah cried.

Boris fell off the table in alarm.

Gently, Mum said, "Boris doesn't like swimming. He's too old and worn out. Just look at him!"

"What do old, worn out people like, then, for a treat?" Benjamin asked.

He had an idea.

"I know! A day at the farm. That's what you had, isn't it, Mum?"

"That was a health farm, Benjamin. It's different," said Mum.

"A health farm," said Benjamin. "What's that?"

"A health farm is somewhere you go to relax," Sarah said.

Boris thought that sounded just the ticket!

"And people fuss over you, and feed you good food, and make you feel great," Mum added.

"Yes, yes!" thought Boris. "That's for me!"

Dad came in from his early morning jog.

"What's going on?" he asked.

"We're going to turn the house into a health

farm today, for Boris's birthday treat," Mum told him.

"Right!" said Dad. "Then we'll need to start with a Computer Profile. Come on, Benjamin."

Dad helped Benjamin make a picture of Boris on the computer. He put in the chewed ear, the broken eye, the crooked arm, and the bald back and tummy.

Then Dad typed out a list of things Boris would need, to make him feel as good as new:

1. Warm soapy soak.
2. Sauna.
3. Brush and rub.
4. Healthy dinner.
5. New ear and eye.
6. Stitch on arm.
7. New fur.

"That should do it," said Dad.

So Benjamin ran a bath for Boris. He put in lots of bubbles. And Boris had a lovely long soak.

When Boris was all clean, and fairly dry, Benjamin looked at the list again.

"How do we do a sauna?" he asked his dad.

"We put Boris in the airing cupboard for an hour or so, and let him steam gently."

After that, Benjamin rubbed Boris's floppy arms and legs, and brushed what was left of his fur. Then they all had carrots and cottage cheese for dinner.

After dinner, Benjamin and Sarah raided the biscuit tin – healthy food didn't seem to have filled them up very much!

Mum repaired Boris's ear, and gave him a new eye. She put a few stitches in his arm, to make it straight.

They all looked at the list. There was only one thing left – new fur. How on earth were they going to do that? But Sarah had spent the day making Boris a new body wig, out of a piece of red fur. He put it on.

He looked wonderful! He felt fabulous! Boris jumped up onto the table, and did a little dance.

"I feel as good as new!" he cried. "Come on, everyone – let's have a party!"

But Benjamin and Sarah and Mum and Dad all groaned. They were quite worn out!

The Very First Blackbird

Kathy Henderson

The Very First Blackbird

Kathy Henderson

Some things are true and some things are stories. And sometimes things that sound like stories turn out to be true after all. It's hard to know.

Jim was a little boy who used to wake up in the night quite often. He'd lie there in the dark and think things or hear things. And sometimes he'd get scared. Then he'd tiptoe to his mother's room.

"There's something there," he'd say.

"Hmmm," she'd mumble, mostly asleep, "What?"

"A rustling" it would be one night.

"A banging" another.

"Elephants!" said Joe one middle of the night when she didn't want to hear.

And usually he'd curl up in her bed and warm his cold feet on her and go back to sleep that way.

But one night, no, very early morning, almost dawn with the first blackbird just starting to sing in the dark, Jim came into his mother's room again.

"I heard something!" he said.

"Hmmm," she mumbled as she always did, mostly asleep. "What?"

"I don't know. A sort of scratching."

"Hmmm," said his mother and she rolled over to make room for him as usual.

But Jim didn't want to get in.

"There's a noise, Mum. Come and listen!"

"Noise," she sighed, putting the pillow over her head.

But Jim wouldn't give up. No. He lifted the pillow, he pleaded and tugged until, in the end, his sleepy mother stumbled up out of bed and along the passage to Jim's own room. She flopped down on the bed and yawned.

Jim's room was just starting to shake off the night. Its clean white walls were coming out of the shadows now and the square shapes hanging on them were turning back from dark holes into pictures. A mirror and a chair reappeared, and a bookshelf with books and tapes and bears and cars, and then two big toy boxes and a cupboard. The first pale light of the early summer sun came creeping in round the edge of the curtains and more birds sang outside. It was peaceful and safe and as quiet as could be.

Jim's mother lay down on his bed and pulled the duvet up over her.

"Aaah!" she said, all cosy, and closed her eyes.

"No Mum, listen!"

They both listened . . .

And heard . . .

Nothing.

Except the first early morning city rumbles, dozy noises, car grumbles, door slams, a nee-naw in the distance, the wind ruffling things and more and more birds singing.

"I can't hear anything," mumbled Jim's mother snuggling her head further into his pillow, three-quarters asleep again already.

"There *is* something there!" said Jim, "I *know* there is!"

He froze. She dozed.

Scrabble! went something.

Jim's mother opened her eyes.

Scrabble! Cheep! went something again.

She sat up.

"See?" said Jim shivering. "There's something there! It scrabbles. It cheeps. It could be a rat! It could be a monster! . . . It could be . . ."

What could it be?

Jim and his mother looked for the noise.

They drew back the curtains and let the light pour in and then they looked all round the room.

They looked into the cupboard,

and under the bed,

through the bookshelves

behind the books and the tapes and the bears round the toy boxes among heaps of furry things and don't-throw-those-aways

and they couldn't find that cheeper anywhere.

They pulled back the covers and riffled through the clothes. They looked outside the windows and behind the door. They looked into and onto and under and over everything until there were only walls and floors and ceilings left and they couldn't find that noise at all.

Cheep! Peep!

Jim's mother sat down on the bed again and cuddled Jim up next to her.

"Don't worry," she said, "we'll just have to listen harder and see if we can hear where it's coming from."

"*Zheep!*" it went again.

Jim pointed to the top of the wall opposite. His mother pointed to the bottom of the cupboard next to it.

"Over there."

"But where?" They crept over to the place and waited again.

Scrabble. Cheep!

This time it was so loud they both jumped.

"It's in there!"

79

"But that's the wall!"

A cheeper in a wall?!

A zeeper in the bricks?!

Jim's mother looked hard at the smooth white wall.

"See that?" she said, and she pointed to six little slits not far up from the bottom. "That's an airbrick. They put them in walls to let air into hollow places. I think there was a fireplace here once and someone's covered it up. And where there's a fireplace there's always a flue, like a tunnel that goes up to the chimney pot so the smoke can get out." She looked at Jim and she wasn't at all sleepy now.

"You know what?" she said. "I think something's fallen down the chimney and into the place where the fireplace used to be behind your wall."

Scrabble. Scrabble went the noise.

"A rat?" asked Jim, shuddering.

"More like a bird," said his mother.

"Can't it get out?"

"No, it's trapped. We'll have to get it out . . . Or it'll die."

"Quick!"

"I know," she said and she got up to leave the room.

"I'm coming with you," said Jim, scuttling

after her quickly. He didn't want to be left behind. Not with a chimney, a fireplace, a hole and something trapped, all behind his quiet white wall! No thankyou!

Cheep!

Down the stairs to the kitchen went Jim's mother, pulling on a sweater and some socks on the way. Down the stairs to the basement. She dug around and found a hammer and a chisel and a screwdriver and some old newspapers and then came all the way back to Jim's room again with Jim running alongside, carrying things.

Zheep!

They could hear it from the top of the stairs. "Hurry!" said Jim.

Cheep! Scrabble!

Together Jim and his mother pushed the furniture out of the way. He spread out the newspapers on the floor. With one hand his mother pressed the chisel into the wall next to the airbrick, with the other she took the hammer and hit the handle of the chisel hard with it. The clean white wall cracked. A chunk of plaster fell out onto the floor. The cheeping stopped.

BANG! TAP! CRASH! CRUNCH!

Jim's mother chipped and chopped round one

side of the airbrick, two sides, three sides and four until *BANG CRASH!* she pulled the whole brick out in a cloud of crusty dust and soot and grit.

There was silence.

Jim and his mother looked into the hole. It was dark in there, very dark. Nothing moved. There wasn't a sound.

Very carefully Jim's mother put her hand into the hollow space behind the hole and felt around.

"I can feel something," she said. "It feels like feathers. It feels quite big. I think it's a bird. But it's stiff . . . It's cold . . . Oh dear," she took her hand out. "I think it's dead."

Jim and his mother sat there on the newspaper full of broken plaster and sooty dust and looked at the wrecked wall and the messed up room. All that to rescue a bird and now it was dead! Jim felt like crying. It was very quiet.

Suddenly there was a whirling and a scrabbling and a shower of soot.

Cheep! Zheep! Cheep!

A very small dirty bundle of panic-stricken feathers whirled out of the hole and past their heads. It flew round and round bumping into the walls and crashing into the lampshade.

The noise seemed loud as thunder. The room seemed small as a cage.

Jim jumped back. His heart was pounding.

"It's alive after all! But it'll hurt itself!"

"Quick! Shut the door so it can't get lost in the house!" said his mother and she ran to the window and threw it open.

Round and round, banging and fluttering *Cheep! Zheep!* flew the dusty little bird until, at last, at last, it flew out of the open window and away into the summer morning, leaving a trail of soot, and Jim and his mother quivering.

"I don't understand," said Jim's mother, "I thought it was dead. I'm sure it was dead. I'm glad it wasn't."

"Did we rescue it?" asked Jim.

"Yes. I think we did."

Jim's mother went back to the hole in the wall and started tidying up the mess.

"It doesn't really make sense," she said, looking puzzled. Jim watched her put her hand into the hole and feel around again.

"Ah!" she said. "Look!" and out she pulled a big bundle of black feathers. It was a dead blackbird she was holding, all dried up, just bone and feather.

"There were two birds, not one," she said.

This one must have fallen down a long time ago and nobody heard."

Jim took the dead blackbird and cuddled it. He looked into the dark hole and he looked out at the sky and he thought of the song that he sometimes heard when he was awake in the night before it was even light. The song of the very first blackbird high on the rooftops.

"Poor thing," said Jim. "Poor thing."

"I'll help you bury it when I've fixed your wall," said his mum, going to fetch filler and paint. "And then we'll have to get someone to come and cover the chimney pot with wire so that no more birds can fall down there."

They buried the stiff dead blackbird in the garden. Jim was sorry to see it go into the ground.

He wondered what else lay behind the skin of the house and his mother wondered which things were stories and which were true.

Shadow

Ann Turnbull

Shadow

Ann Turnbull

Shadow lived in Bill's garden, but she was not Bill's cat. She was a stray cat, shy of people.

It was Bill who named her Shadow.

"Because you're so quiet and secret," he said, "and yet whenever I turn round, there you are: my shadow cat."

"I'm not your cat," said Shadow.

But she liked to be near Bill when he was gardening. Sometimes she dozed in the catmint, with the sun warm on her fur; sometimes she kept cool under the laurel bush;

sometimes she watched the frogspawn twitching in the pond. If Bill was digging she would come and scratch in the crumbly earth.

But she would not let Bill touch her. She hissed if he came too close. Shadow was shy of people, even Bill.

"I don't know what you live on," said Bill.

He put out food and milk for Shadow, near the back door. Shadow drank the milk and ate the food and licked the plates clean, but although Bill always left the door half open, she never came in.

"You need somewhere to go when it's raining," said Bill.

He opened a window in the shed so that Shadow could slip inside.

By day the garden was Bill's; by night it was Shadow's.

"I wonder what you do all night," said Bill.

Shadow looked at him with round gold eyes. She said, "I watch the moon through a net of leaves. I fish for stars in puddles. Mice go skittering through the grass and turn to dry leaves in my paws. Strange cats come. I stare them out; stare outstare till they slink away. This is my garden. No cat hunts here but me."

Spring turned the garden green. Daffodils

bloomed. Frogs hopped and splashed in the pond and Shadow splashed after them.

"Have to get planting soon," said Bill.

But then came snow: sudden snow that piled up deep drifts beneath the apple tree and under the rockery. The daffodils' petals were clogged, the pond sealed in ice.

Shadow hated the snow. It soaked her fur and stung her eyes. She lifted each paw in turn and shook it.

All night it snowed, and all the next day. Shadow went to the shed, but the catch on the window had dropped shut in the wind and she could not get in.

She sat under the laurel bush and waited.

In the evening Bill put out her food. Shadow ran to meet him.

"You're wet, lass!" He tried to stroke her, but Shadow shrank away. "Come on, then. Eat your dinner. I'll go back in the warm."

But he left the door open, just a crack. And when she had eaten, Shadow felt the warmth of the house calling to her. She put a paw on the door sill.

"Come in, Shadow," Bill said.

Shadow crept inside.

Her ears went back at the hiss of the gas fire, but its warmth was kind. She felt the hearth rug soft under her paws.

"I'm not a house cat," said Shadow, "but I will stay here tonight."

She listened to the ticking of Bill's clock and the creak of his chair. The sounds were comforting. She purred and fell asleep.

The next night Shadow came in again. This time she was bolder. She sprang onto the television and up to the mantelpiece and picked her way between the clock and the silver-framed photograph of Bill's wife, Margaret, and then down again onto the back of Bill's chair.

"Shadow," said Bill, "you're all alone out there, and I'm all alone in here. We could be company, us two."

Shadow looked at him with round gold eyes. She said, "I am not a house cat. My place is in the garden. I guard the pond where the star frogs leap at night; I know their hiding places under the lilies. I stalk birds at dawn and leave my paw prints in the dew. I don't need company."

But after that night, whenever the wind was cold or rain was falling, Shadow would scratch at the back door to come in. Then she would sit in the warm room with Bill and his television and the photograph of Margaret, and Bill would listen to her purring.

Shadow began to lose her fear. She let Bill stroke her. She rubbed her head against his knees. And one day she jumped on his lap and purred and plucked with needle claws.

Bill smiled and stroked her. "Everyone needs company," he said.

Spelling Lesson

Helen Cresswell

Spelling Lesson

Helen Cresswell

Victoria Lucy Emmett was six years eight months and two days old when it happened. (Most people can't remember when they learned to spell, but she can.) She lived at number six Meadow Lane with her father and mother and brother Ben. He was eight years and goodness knows how many months and days. He called his sister Sicky Vicky when he felt like it, and she called him Clever Clogs.

Victoria believed in magic. She believed in witches, genies in bottles, gingerbread houses and giants. Ben didn't.

"You'd better watch out!" she told him. "Don't you even believe in *wishes*?"

"They don't work," he told her. "Last birthday I wished for a new bike till I nearly *bust*, and I still didn't get one. Wishes are rubbish."

"What about spells? Don't you even believe in spells?"

"No such thing," he said. "Why don't you grow up, Sicky Vicky?"

"Oh *you*, Clever Clogs! You'd better watch out!"

And off she went to make a spell. She didn't really know where to start, having never made a spell before.

"You need a recipe," she thought, "and you need special words. Recipe first. Pity a witch doesn't live next door."

Who actually lived next door was Miss Drake, who was amazingly old and had a black cat called Graymalkin. She grew herbs in her tiny garden and dried them in her kitchen. She was definitely the next best thing to a witch.

Victoria went round and knocked on her door. Miss Drake opened it. She was wearing black, as usual.

"Good morning, Miss Drake," said Victoria politely.

"It might be," replied Miss Drake. "We shall have to see."

"I just wondered if you had some herbs to spare," said Victoria. "I want to make a spell."

"A ssspell . . ." repeated Miss Drake, in a hissing kind of way. She smiled, and her face cracked into a thousand wrinkles. Her eyes, which were green, glittered. "There's a pretty thought, my dear. You had better come in."

So for the first time Victoria went into the poky little house, down a dark passage and into the kitchen. Bunches of herbs hung from hooks. Graymalkin lay by the fire growling, and above the fire was a large black cauldron. It bubbled and simmered and steamed and certainly did not smell like anyone's dinner.

"A ssspell . . ." said Miss Drake again. "What kind of a spell? Go invisible . . . fly through the air . . . turn toad?"

"*That's* an idea!" said Victoria, who hadn't

really thought what the spell would be. "Turn toad!"

"Who?" enquired Miss Drake. "You?"

"Oh no!" said Victoria hastily. "Ben! You know – the one who's always kicking balls into your garden. *And* he doesn't believe in magic."

"Ah!" said Miss Drake. "Him!"

"Thinks he knows everything," Victoria told her. "Clever Clogs. Serve him right to be turned toad. Have you got some good things to mix up?"

Miss Drake had. The pair prepared the mixture together. Victoria ground the herbs with a pestle and mortar, while Miss Drake carefully ladled the liquid from the cauldron and measured dark tinctures from a row of bottles on the shelves.

"What does your brother like to drink?" she asked.

"Well, he quite likes coffee, but Mum doesn't let him have it very often," said Victoria. "She says it's bad for him. *She* drinks it though, lots of it."

Miss Drake let Victoria tip her herbs into the mixture, then heated it in a saucepan. It

looked – and funnily enough smelled – exactly like coffee.

"Shouldn't there be a frog's leg?" asked Victoria. "Or hair of cat? And what about the words?"

"Oh, that's the easy part," Miss Drake told her, and began to mumble and mutter as she stirred. Victoria couldn't catch the words, but they sounded quite spellish.

"There!" Miss Drake poured the steaming mixture into a blue mug. "Quickly, now, before it gets cold!"

Victoria picked up the mug and carried it carefully through to the passage and Miss Drake opened the front door to let her out. Back home, Victoria could see her mother in the garden, weeding. On the kitchen table stood a steaming mug of coffee.

"Better find Ben quickly, before Mum sees," she thought. She put her own mug down and went to fetch him. He was making a kite from a kit.

"Toads don't fly kites," Victoria thought, "so *I* shall be able to have it."

"*What?*" he said when she told him. "Coffee? You're barmy. Any case, you're not allowed to muck around with the stove. *Or* the kettle."

She hadn't thought of that. She began to wish she had chosen orange juice instead of coffee. On the other hand, surely even clever Miss Drake could not have made *that* concoction look and taste like orange juice.

"Well anyway, I did," she said. "Come *on*."

"No fear!" said Ben. "It's a trick."

"It is not!"

" 'Tis."

" 'T'isn't."

" 'Tis."

" 'T'isn't."

Victoria felt quite desperate. It looked as though a perfectly good spell was going to waste.

"I bet you it isn't!" she said.

He looked at her.

"Bet me what?"

"Bet you . . . bet you . . ." she couldn't for the life of her think what.

"Your pocket money?" he suggested.

She did not hesitate. It would easily be worth fifty pence to see Ben turned toad.

"All right," she said. "Come *on*!"

He got up and followed her downstairs. Her

103

heart went hammer hammer hammer. Now it was going to happen. Clever Clogs would turn toad under her very eyes.

"There!" She pushed open the kitchen door and pointed triumphantly at the mug of steaming coffee. Ben boggled.

"You'll catch it if mum finds out!" was all he said.

"Go on then – drink it!"

"Still think it's fishy. Bet you've put salt in it."

"No I have not! Taste it!"

He picked up the coffee. Her heart went hammer hammer hammer. He sipped it. He sipped again. Victoria held her breath.

"Not bad," he said grudgingly.

He was still Ben, not a toad. Perhaps he had to drink all of it?

He fetched the biscuit tin and sat down. Victoria watched him.

She did not take her eyes off him for a single instant. She did not want to miss the actual, magical moment when he would turn toad.

"Where's Mum?" he asked, dunking a biscuit.

"In the garden."

"Dunno what she'll say, if she—"

He stopped. He stared. His eyes bulged.

"This is it!" she thought. "He's turning!"

Toads have bulging eyes.

He went on boggling. His mug went down plonk on the table, his mouth opened and closed but no sound came out.

"Perhaps he can only croak now," Victoria thought. "But why's he not shrinking? And why's he not going all brown and leathery?"

He pointed. She turned. She boggled. Her mouth opened and closed but no sound came out.

There, squatting by the sink, was a huge toad. It was brown and khaki with eyes like marbles. Its mouth opened and closed but no sound came out.

"Oh help!" said Victoria faintly.

Ben pushed back his chair and ran to the back door.

"Mum!" he yelled. "Quick!" Silence. Then, "She's not there. Thought you said she was in the garden."

Victoria's eyes travelled up from the squatting toad to the draining board. There, empty, was a blue mug.

105

She looked at the toad.

"Oh Mum!" she whispered. "What've I done?"

The toad looked mournfully back at her.

"Dirty great thing!" said Ben. "How did it get in here?"

"It's Mum!" said Victoria. Her voice came out all squeaky.

"You *what*?"

"It's Mum. Oh Mum, I didn't mean it!"

Ben seized the sweeping brush propped by the door.

"Look out!"

"No!" screamed Victoria. "Don't! You'll hurt her!"

She grabbed hold of the handle and tried to pull it away. This way and that they tugged while the toad sat watching with glassy eyes.

"It's Mum, it really is, it's Mum!"

"Idiot – give it *here*!"

"I did a spell – it was meant for you! *You* should be a toad!"

Ben let go of the brush.

"Go on then," he said. "Spit it out."

So she told him. She told him about her visit

to Miss Drake, and how the two of them had mixed the spell together.

"And I meant it to be *you*!" she wailed.

"Thank you very much," he said.

"And now we've got a toad for a mother! What'll we do, what'll we do?"

"You're making the whole thing up," Ben said. "Must be. No such thing as spells."

"That's what you always say!"

"Mum's about somewhere. She wouldn't just go out and leave us. Mum! Mum!"

In the silence that followed the toad made a little series of jumps forward – hop hop hop!

"Oh help!" Ben said. "It heard me!" He backed away.

"*Now* do you believe me? I don't like it, I don't like it!"

And Victoria began to cry. Her own dear mother was now a hideous toad and it was all her fault.

"Cry baby," Ben said. "It's no use blubbing. Dad'll kill you when he gets home. Are you *sure* it's her? No such thing as spells."

This time, he didn't sound quite so certain.

"If there *were* such things as spells," he went on, "I suppose there must be a way of *un*spelling them."

Victoria stopped crying. She stared, first at the toad with its pulsing double chin, then at Ben.

"*I* don't know how," she said, "but perhaps Miss Drake does."

"Well you'd better get round there fast and ask her," he told her.

Victoria hesitated. Miss Drake had been all very well when she *was* Miss Drake. Now it looked as if she were a real live witch.

"You'll have to come with me," she said.

"I'll stop and keep an eye on *that*. If it hops off, we're sunk."

"We can shut the doors to keep it in. I'm not going by myself."

"Oh, all *right*!" He banged shut the door that led to the hall.

"You stop there, ugly mug!" he told the toad.

They both went out of the back door and shut it behind them. Next door, Victoria took a deep breath and knocked.

The door opened. Miss Drake looked from one to the other.

"I'm sorry to trouble you Miss Drake this is Ben!" said Victoria, all in one breath.

"Hmph!" said Miss Drake, and her green eyes narrowed. "Not a toad, then. Why?"

"I – I – it all went wrong," Victoria stammered.

Miss Drake held the door wide.

"You'd better come in."

Back in the tiny kitchen, with Graymalkin still growling and the cauldron still bubbling, Victoria told her story.

"It was a lovely spell, it really was, and it worked," she finished, "but it got the wrong person."

"*You* got the wrong person," Miss Drake corrected. She fixed Ben with her greeny yellowy eyes. "*You* should be a toad!"

He did not reply.

"Don't believe in spells, eh?"

Still he did not reply. He did not even shake his head.

"No he doesn't!" Victoria said. "*Or* witches, *or* wishes, *or* giants! He doesn't believe in *anything*!"

Now there was a very long silence, but for the growling cat and the bubbling cauldron.

"Don't believe must be *made* to believe!" The words were a fierce hiss.

"Oh, don't turn him toad as well!" Victoria wailed. A toad for mother *and* brother would be too much to bear.

"I just wondered . . . I just wondered . . . oh, can't you turn her back?"

"*I* can't," said Miss Drake. "But perhaps you can. Or perhaps . . . you!"

She looked at Ben, and grinned. Her face splintered like glass.

"Yessss . . . yesss . . . you!"

"Shall we make another spell?" asked Victoria. The first one might have gone wrong, but she had enjoyed making it just the same.

"Oh no . . . oh no . . . that's not the way . . ."

"W-what, then?"

Miss Drake shook her head and the grey wisps flew.

"Don't you know your fairy tales? Think, child, think!"

Victoria thought as hard as she knew how, she thought till her brain ached.

"The Frog Prince!" Miss Drake hissed.

Then Victoria remembered. The story of the princess who threw her golden ball into the well, and a frog fetched it out and went to live with her at the palace. That frog ate with her and slept with her and in the end—

"Oh!" she gasped. "Oh no!"

The princess at last had had to *kiss* that frog before he could change back into a handsome prince. Victoria did not think she could kiss that toad. In fact, she *knew* she couldn't.

"I can't!" she wailed. "Oh – I can't!"

"Not you," said Miss Drake calmly. "*Him*!"

Ben looked from one to the other of them. He had not the foggiest idea what they were talking about. He played computer games instead of reading fairy tales.

"He shall do it!" said Miss Drake. "Perhaps then we shall see who doesn't believe in spells! Tell him, child!"

Victoria gulped. An hour ago she had wanted him turned toad. Now she was actually feeling sorry for him. He would have to go down on his hands and knees and put his face forward right up against that pimply brown skin and those bulging eyes and—

"Ugh!" she shuddered at the very thought.

"Tell him," repeated Miss Drake.

So Victoria did, in a trembly voice. Still Ben did not say anything. He had not said a single word since they had come into Miss Drake's house and he had begun to suspect, for the first time in his life, that there might be such things as spells – and witches. He did go pale, though. He went very white indeed.

"*Kisss* it!" said Miss Drake hissingly. "Kissss it! It's the only way."

"It is, Ben, it's true. It might not be too bad. You can just shut your eyes and just – ever so quickly – and it is Mum, remember!"

Ben turned. He marched out of the kitchen and down the passage and Victoria hurried

after him. As they went into the street Miss
Drake's triumphant voice followed them:

"Don't believe must be made to believe!
Kisss kisss kisss!"

And that is exactly what Ben did. Back in
the kitchen, the toad still squatted exactly
where they had left it. Ben got down on his
hands and knees. He drew an enormous
breath and shut his eyes and—

Kiss – whoosh!

It happened so fast that Victoria almost
missed it by blinking.

"Oh *do* get from under my feet, Ben!" said
Mrs Emmett. "Have you lost something?"

He had – almost. His own mother.

"Funny . . ." she was looking at the table
now, and the mug of coffee, no longer
steaming. "I could've sworn I'd drunk that . . ."

"She doesn't remember!" thought Victoria.
"Oh, thank goodness!"

Then she noticed the empty blue mug on
the draining board. Quick as a flash she picked
it up and put it behind her back.

"I want you to go to the shop for me, Ben,"
her mother was saying.

"I'll go with him!" Victoria said.

They would have to take the blue mug back to Miss Drake. She would have to knock, for the third time that morning, on a witch's door.

"And after that," she thought, "I don't think I'll go there again."

Victoria Lucy Emmett had had her first and last spelling lesson. Witches and spells were all very well, she decided, but on the whole they were better kept in story books, where they belong.

Uproar in Yukland

Leon Rosselson

Uproar in Yukland

Leon Rosselson

Underneath the floorboards live the Yuks. Creaky creatures they are with goggle eyes and teeth like macaroni sticks. You may see them as you tiptoe to the fridge on a sleepless summer's night in search of a midnight snack of raspberry jelly and chocolate chip ice cream. And if you do catch sight of them popping up through the cracks in the floorboards, you may wonder how it is possible to tell one Yuk from another Yuk. Because all Yuks look the same. They dress the same. They smell the same. They *are* the same.

Except, of course, for Anton Yuk.

Every morning, at the first croak of the froghorn, the Yuks leap as one out of their mudbags, wash themselves thoroughly in tubs of glue and breakfast on squashed fly sandwiches and mugs of slime tea which they stir with the ends of their noses.

But not Anton Yuk. He lies lazily in a smelly bubbly bath, munching a mouthful of apple pips.

After breakfast, all the Yuks stand to attention and sing the Yuk anthem. This consists of repeating the word YUK in tuneless unison over and over again until they all fall to the ground in a kind of trance.

But not Anton Yuk. He prefers to whistle a trilling tune that he has made up himself.

This does not please the other Yuks. "Anton is bad," they cry. "Anton is disobedient. Be careful, Anton, or you will be punished."

Worst of all, Anton refuses to respect the Yuk greeting. When one Yuk meets another Yuk in the dusty alleyways beneath the floorboards, the polite and proper thing for them to do is to bang their heads together hard and often until both of them crash to the floor unconscious. Don't ask me why they do that. That is what they do and that is what they have always done since the beginning of time and no Yuk has ever thought to question it.

Until Anton Yuk. Anton Yuk, by way of greeting, holds out a hand to be shaken and murmurs "How do you do?"

The other Yuks are shocked. "This is an insult to our sacred customs," they say.

"Besides, shaking hands and saying 'How do you do?' is daft."

"It may be daft," retorts Anton, "but at least it's different. And," he adds, "it doesn't give you a headache."

And so one doomful day, Anton Yuk was brought before the Yuk Elders (or Yackety Yuks, as they were called) and accused of trying to be different. The Yackety Yuks sat on piles of bones in Horatio Yuk Hall which was named after the great Yuk hero who had invented glue. A giant statue of Horatio Yuk bathing in a tub of glue stood in the square outside.

"Your disobedience must be punished," the Yackety Yuks decided. "You will be bound in iron chains and locked deep down in a dark and dismal dungeon until you grovel for forgiveness."

"That'll be the day," said Anton Yuk.

The Yuk Elders, according to their ancient custom, squeezed their noses between their thumbs and forefingers and pronounced (nasally): "We have spoken."

So they took Anton away and bound him in iron chains and locked him deep down in a dark and dismal dungeon. And every morning, the guard brought him his breakfast of slime tea and squashed fly sandwiches. And every evening, another guard (or could it have been the same guard because it's impossible to tell one Yuk from another Yuk) brought him his supper of spider soup and burnt maggot pie.

And every so often, the Yuk Elders sent a messenger to ask if he was ready to grovel for forgiveness.

"That'll be the day," Anton would reply.

So a week passed, or it could have been a month or even a year because being locked deep down in a dark and dismal dungeon made Anton lose all sense of time. It also made him very hungry. He hated slime tea and squashed fly sandwiches and spider soup and especially burnt maggot pie. He left most of it for the guard to gollop down greedily.

What's more he was bored with being bound in iron chains. He wanted to bathe in a smelly bubbly bath. He wanted to munch a mouthful of apple pips. He wanted to be free. But he didn't want to grovel for forgiveness. What was he to do?

"Yukky!" belched the guard one morning

after he'd polished off Anton's breakfast. "Squashed fly sandwiches are my favourite."

"Can I have some apple pips?" asked Anton.

"Forbidden," said the guard.

"Just a mouthful," pleaded Anton.

The goggle-eyed guard glared.

"I'll tell you a joke," Anton said.

"What's a joke?" asked the guard.

"I say something funny and you laugh," explained Anton.

The guard's goggle eyes nearly popped out of his head. "Yuks don't laugh," he said.

It was true. No Yuks had ever been known to laugh. Except Anton Yuk, of course. But doing things that no Yuk had ever been known to do was what had got him into this mess in the first place.

"It'll make you feel delumptious," Anton said, "laughing will."

"What's delumptious?" asked the guard.

"You'll see," said Anton.

"All right," said the guard because he, too, was bored and he thought feeling delumptious might make a change.

So the guard gave Anton a mouthful of apple pips and Anton told the guard this joke.

"Two Yuks were walking along the alley-ways underneath the floorboards. One Yuk fell down a yukhole. The first Yuk shouted down to the Yuk who'd fallen, 'Is it dark down there?' The second Yuk called back, 'I don't know. I can't see a thing.' "

The guard thought about this joke for a minute. Then he said, "I don't feel very delumptious."

"You haven't laughed yet," explained Anton.

"How do you laugh?" asked the guard.

"Ha, ha," said Anton.

"Ha, ha," said the guard.

"Ha, ha, ha," said Anton.

"Ha, ha, ha," repeated the guard.

"Ha, ha, ha, ha, ha, ha," said Anton.

"Ha, ha, ha, ha, ha, ha," echoed the guard.

"Don't stop," said Anton.

"Ha, ha, ha . . ."

Gradually the laughter took hold of the guard, took hold of him body and bone and then heart and soul. He showed his macaroni teeth. He wibbled and wobbled like raspberry jelly. He rolled around the floor. In short, he laughed fit to bust.

"How do you feel?" asked Anton when the

guard had recovered himself.

"Delumptious," said the guard.

"Told you," said Anton. "Want one of my apple pips?"

The next day, another guard brought Anton his breakfast and Anton made the same bargain with him. Apple pips for a joke. That's how it began. Soon all the guards, not wanting to be left out, were asking Anton to tell them jokes so they, too, could feel delumptious. Laughter was spreading through the Yuk nation.

The Yuk Elders were puzzled. Not only were many Yuks going about with mad grins on their faces and showing their macaroni-stick teeth but Anton was still refusing to grovel for forgiveness.

"That'll be the day," was all he would say.

Another week passed (or it could have been a month or even a year). The guard (whichever it was and it doesn't really matter because all Yuks look the same) brought Anton his breakfast and offered him apple pips in exchange for a joke.

"Thank you," said Anton, "but I know a way to make you feel doubly delumptious."

"What's that feel like?" asked the guard.

"You'll see," said Anton. "First unbind my arms and legs from these iron chains."

"Forbidden," said the guard.

"You'll feel doubly delumptious," promised Anton.

"Oh all right," said the guard. So he did.

Once unbound, Anton held out his hand to be shaken and murmured "How do you do?"

The guard frowned. "That's daft," he said.

"You'll feel doubly delumptious," said Anton.

The guard hesitated. Then, feeling silly, he shook Anton's hand and said: "How do you do?"

"How do you feel?" asked Anton.

"Silly," said the guard.

"Keep practising," said Anton. "You'll get used to it. And then you'll feel—"

"I know," said the guard. "Doubly delumptious."

So the guard kept practising. At first he felt awkward holding out his hand to be shaken and murmuring "How do you do?" when all the other Yuks were banging their heads together. But he soon got used to it. What's more, the bumps on his head disappeared and the pains in his head vanished. In fact, he felt doubly delumptious.

Soon other Yuks began to adopt this new form of greeting just as they had the jokes and the laughter. Arguments arose between these newfanglers, as they were called, and the mudstickers who wanted to follow the old ways.

The Yuk Elders were worried. Not only was Anton Yuk not grovelling for forgiveness but disobedience was breaking out everywhere.

More and more Yuks joined the followers of Anton. They waited eagerly for his next new idea. They began bathing in smelly bubbly baths instead of tubs of glue. It made them feel, they said, doubly doubly delumptious. Then while the mudstickers were singing the old Yuk anthem, the newfanglers started whistling the trilling tune that Anton Yuk had made up himself. What a cacophony!

The Yuk nation was in an uproar. No-one knew what was right or wrong any more. Something had to be done.

And it was. The Yackety Yuks, the Yuk Elders, held an emergency meeting in Horatio

Yuk Hall. The Yuks gathered in the square outside and waited with bated breath. Some of them held their breath for so long they collapsed and had to be carted off to hospital to be revived.

At the day's end, the Yuk Elders sent out a messenger to announce their judgement. This is what they decided. Firstly, all Yuks were now to greet each other by holding out their hands to be shaken and murmuring "How do you do?" instead of all that headbanging. Secondly, all Yuks were to wash in smelly bubbly baths instead of tubs of glue. Thirdly, apple pips were to be munched for breakfast. Fourthly, the old Yuk anthem would no longer be sung. Instead, Anton Yuk's tune would be whistled. Fifthly and lastly, since Anton Yuk was now doing exactly what every other Yuk would be doing, he could no longer be accused of trying to be different. He was to be released at once.

And so order was restored in Yukland. Anton Yuk was released from the dark and dismal dungeon to ear-splitting cries of "Hip hip hooyuki!" The Yuk Elders held out their hands and murmured "How do you do?" And in time, Anton Yuk himself was chosen to be a Yackety Yuk.

And that's why if you do happen to see any Yuks as you tiptoe to the fridge on a sleepless summer's night in search of a midnight snack of raspberry jelly and chocolate chip ice cream, if you do chance to catch sight of any Yuks popping up through the cracks in the floorboards, you will not be able to tell one Yuk from another Yuk. Because all Yuks look the same. They dress the same. They smell the same. They *are* the same.

Except, of course, for Winifred Yuk.

But that's another story.

Rupert the
Second

Mary Rayner

Rupert the Second

Mary Rayner

Before Andrew went skating, he went upstairs to check that the snake was still asleep in its box on the window sill.

It was a grass snake. Andrew was looking after it through the school holidays. Not a difficult job, since the snake had gone into its winter sleep some time ago. All that Andrew had to do was keep it cool, and make sure it was all right now and then.

Mr Carpenter, Andrew's teacher, had been going away over Christmas. The snake could not be left in the classroom through the holidays, Mr Carpenter had said. You never knew what the cleaners might do to it, they might mistake it for an adder.

Andrew now knew the difference between an adder and a grass snake. They had different markings, and a grass snake was not poisonous.

Andrew lifted the lid of the box. The snake was coiled round in exactly the same position as the last time he had looked.

"Hello, snake," said Andrew. It needed a name. On the bed was Andrew's battered old teddy, Rupert. That would be a good name for a snake. But perhaps a bit unfair on the teddy? All right then, Rupert the Second.

"Andrew, we're waiting," his sister Liz called up the stairs. Andrew put half a biscuit in the box, just in case Rupert the Second should wake up feeling hungry while he was out skating, shut the lid and thundered downstairs.

"About time," said Elaine, his oldest sister. Tomorrow was Christmas Day. It was

Mum's idea that they should walk round to
the skating rink. "Elaine can help you two
with your boots," she'd said. "I don't want you
all under foot. There's the turkey to stuff and
everything to get ready for James and
Kathleen and all their lot coming to Christmas
dinner. And there won't be time tomorrow
morning, because of opening the presents and
then church. Oh and I nearly forgot. The new
vicar's having a blessing ceremony at the
Family Service, and he wants all of you
children to bring your favourite toys and
animals. Teddies and things."

I'll take Rupert, thought Andrew as he broke
into a run to keep up with Elaine.

Next morning there were some wonderful
presents. A brand new football for Andrew,
and a Manchester United outfit, and many
more. Andrew tried on the outfit at once. It
fitted, and looked great. He wanted to have a
go with the football, but in no time at all Dad
was telling them to get ready for church, and
Mum was asking if everybody'd got their
things.

Andrew scrambled out of his football gear

and back into his ordinary clothes. He tore upstairs to fetch Rupert.

He was fairly sure that Mum and Dad would say no if he asked, so he opened the box and lifted the snake out carefully. If he undid the zip of his anorak pocket, he could fit him in quite snugly, no one would know. And by the time they reached church it would be all right, because God would know he was a grass snake and not harmful, God knew everything.

In the back of the car Andrew sat up very straight between Liz and Elaine so as not to squash Rupert. They all walked up the centre aisle of the church and sat down in a pew.

Over in one corner was the crib, with a spotlight shining down on it, and candles behind, and wooden figures of Mary and Joseph and the Baby Jesus, the shepherds and the kings, with real straw on the floor. There were more candles fixed to each pillar the whole length of the church, a lot of holly and ivy, and some white flowers up at the top end.

There were a great many people. Andrew had never seen the church so full. It was hot, but he did not dare take off his anorak. He could feel himself going red in the face, but he hoped no one would notice.

They sang several carols, including *The First Noel*. Andrew thought happily about his football, and really let rip on the *Noels*, until Liz dug him in the ribs and hissed "Don't shout."

At last it was time to go up to the altar rail with the other children. Elaine had her china cat, and Liz her fashion doll, and all the others were carrying their toys.

"What about yours?" whispered Mum. "Did you forget?"

137

Andrew patted his pocket. "No, I've got Rupert here."

"Good boy." Mum smiled down at him.

Elaine and Liz edged out along the pew and led the way up the centre aisle. Andrew followed. They went up the steps and knelt down at the altar rail with all the other children. Behind them, in the body of the church, a baby started to cry, its voice echoing up to the rafters.

The vicar moved along. He was holding out his hands in blessing and smiling what Andrew thought was a soppy smile. He was putting his hands on Elaine's head, and then looking fondly down at her china cat while his lips moved.

The baby's wails changed to a steady yelling. The vicar blessed Liz and her doll, then he moved sideways to face Andrew.

Andrew opened the zip, lifted out Rupert with one hand, and held him up. He uncoiled and hung down. Suddenly he seemed awfully big. So long, now that Andrew was kneeling, that he almost touched the floor.

The baby stopped. There was complete silence in the church. The vicar gave a loud gasp and took several steps backward. In the next instant the baby began again, and Liz screamed.

Andrew scowled at her. Trust her not to know a grass snake when she saw one. But there was no time to say anything to her, because she jumped up and disappeared down the steps back to the pew. Andrew kept his gaze on the vicar.

The vicar was mumbling something, one hand held out towards Andrew, but he was some distance away. Why doesn't he come up and put a hand on my head, wondered Andrew, like he did for Elaine and Liz? But the vicar moved on quickly to the next kneeling child.

Goodness, thought Andrew, how white he looks. Christmas must be very hard work for vicars. Tiring. He gave the vicar an understanding smile. Then he rose to his feet, tucking Rupert inside his anorak as best he could, and swung round.

Down in the main church he could see the baby's mother standing up, jiggling the baby up and down. But nothing would still its roars, so she tiptoed out to the door, which clonked

behind her. Anyone could have told her it was
silly to bring a baby to church, thought
Andrew. No idea how to behave. Now Rupert
was another matter.

He walked back to the pew smiling so
happily that his mum asked him what he was
so pleased about.

She was no wiser when he answered.

"The blessing. It worked. God woke him up
to hear it."

On the way out of church, Andrew was
thinking about his three cousins who were
coming to dinner, and his new football. All his
cousins were boys, which was a good thing.
There should be time for a proper game after
dinner.

It took ages getting out of the church, there
were so many people, all squashed against
each other. At the door Andrew felt in his
anorak to make sure Rupert was still all right.
He wasn't there.

They had reached the car before Andrew
could make his mother listen. "It's Rupert.
He's gone."

"I expect he's on the pew seat," said his

father. "Don't worry, no one will take an old teddy."

Andrew was desperate. "No, you don't understand. He could crawl off, he could be stolen, he could be *killed*!"

Liz said nastily, "Serves you right for taking a snake to church."

"A *what*?" said his mum.

"A snake," said Liz.

His mum turned on him. "You brought the *snake*?"

Andrew said, "But you told us to bring our most special toys or animals."

"Oh Andrew. She meant toy animals, not real ones," said his father.

"Of course I thought you had the bear," said his mother. "We can't go back and look now, the turkey will burn and James and Kathleen and the three boys will be waiting outside our house."

His father said, "He can't have gone far. Better to look this afternoon, when the church is empty."

"I really cannot face the new vicar to tell him we've let a snake loose in his church," said his mum.

"What's *wrong* with a snake?" asked Andrew. "I keep telling everybody, he's not dangerous."

"That's not the point," snapped his mother, getting in behind the wheel, revving up the engine and pulling out into the road with unusual speed. She seemed pretty upset.

The turkey wasn't burnt, and Uncle James and Aunt Kathleen and the cousins had only been waiting five minutes when they reached home. Christmas dinner was terrific, or it would have been if only Rupert hadn't been missing, thought Andrew.

At last, when the last piece of Christmas pudding had been eaten by Uncle James, the last cracker pulled, the last cup of coffee drunk by the grown-ups, and Uncle James and Dad were stretched out in chairs on either side of the fire half asleep, Andrew followed his mother into the kitchen.

"Please? *Now* can we go and look for Rupert?"

Aunt Kathleen said, "I'll go. You've done enough. Come on Andrew, you can show me the way. I'll come with you."

The two of them hurried back to the church on foot. Luckily the door was not locked, and they slipped inside. The candles were no longer alight, and the church was much colder. Over in the far corner, the spotlight still shone down on the crib, on the Christ Child in the manger, on the wooden donkey and the shepherds, on Mary and Joseph and the three kings.

They started by trying to find the pew where Andrew had sat. Andrew wished now that his mum had come. He wasn't sure which one it had been.

Aunt Kathleen was very helpful, saying, "Well, never mind, we'll look under them all," but they couldn't find Rupert anywhere.

They looked where all the ivy and holly was twined around the pulpit, they looked in all the corners, they looked by the font, but he wasn't there. Andrew lay on his tummy and looked under the chest where the prayer books were kept, but he wasn't there.

They even went up the altar steps, and lifted up the cloth and looked under the altar, but he wasn't there either.

Aunt Kathleen said at last, "I don't think we're going to find him."

143

"But we've *got* to," said Andrew. "I *promised* to look after him."

Aunt Kathleen said, "One last look."

Andrew said, "D'you think God might help us find him?"

Aunt Kathleen said with a sigh, "I'm not sure that God—" but Andrew was already back across the church to the crib.

He screwed up his eyes and said, out loud, "Jesus, please let me find Rupert. After all," he added, "it was your fault for waking him up."

He opened his eyes and looked down, and there, in shadow, coiled up again and quite still on the flagstone floor, half hidden under one of the pews, was the snake. Fast asleep.

With a cry of joy Andrew gathered him up and put him in his anorak pocket, properly inside this time, and did up the zip.

"There, I told you we'd find him."

When they returned to Andrew's house the others were just starting tea. It was too dark for football now, but never mind, thought Andrew, it had been much more important to look for the snake.

"Did you find him?" asked Uncle James, his mouth full of Christmas cake. "Whatsisname. Rupert?"

"Yes," said Andrew, going upstairs to put him back in his box. "But he's not called Rupert now. He's called Noel, because he's a Christmas snake. Noel the First."

The Stinky Tree

David Henry Wilson

The Stinky Tree

David Henry Wilson

You've never heard of a stinky tree, have you? It's not surprising, because there's no such thing. But there *was* such a thing once, and you can think yourself lucky that you never went near it.

The stinky tree smelt like a combination of a gorilla's armpits after twelve rounds with the heavyweight champion, your feet after you've run twenty miles on a hot day, and a cow's bottom ten seconds after a stomach upset. Only it smelt even worse than that, if you can imagine *anything* smelling worse than that.

Now you might not have realised it, but trees are actually the kindest creatures in the world. They give away their fruit, they provide shelter for all kinds of birds, animals and insects, they supply us with wood and leaf mould, they help to balance air and water, and they look beautiful. If ever a creature deserved a medal for good nature, it's the tree.

But there's always someone somewhere who tries to spoil things, and the stinky tree was that someone.

"Why should I give my fruit away?" he cried. "I grew it, so it's mine. And why should all you birds, animals and insects twitter, munch and grub all over me? I'm private property, that's what I am, and I belong to me, not to you. So go away!"

He said this on a Monday morning. Nobody knew quite why he suddenly decided to become a nasty tree, but Mondays can do funny things to people, so maybe they do funny things to trees as well.

Now before this fateful Monday morning, the stinky tree was not stinky at all. It was a perfectly normal tree, with blossoms in the spring, fruit in the summer, and no problems. The problems started when it told the birds, animals and insects to go away.

"But we live here!" they all whistled, squeaked or buzzed. "This is our home!"

"You lived here," said the tree, "and it was your home. Now you don't and it's not. Whistle, squeak and buzz off."

"Where will we go?"

"That's not my concern. My concern is me. Goodbye."

So the birds, animals and insects flew, ran and crawled off into the next field to hold a conference.

"What are we going to dowoowoowoo?" asked the owl.

"I shall just go nuts," squeaked the squirrel.

"And I shall go round the bend," said the caterpillar.

Of course there were plenty of trees in the neighbourhood, but they all seemed pretty full, and a quick call to the Ministry of Nesting revealed that there was in fact a shortage of accommodation in the area.

"There are no empty trees ariaound," said the official (who was a bureaucat). "You'll have to nest on the griaound."

But everyone knew that ground nesting was far too dangerous. The bureaucat knew it as well, which might be why he suggested it.

Fortunately the trees themselves were much more sympathetic, and before long, offers were coming in:

"I'll take one," said a plum.

"Give me two," said a yew.

"And I can take three," said a horse-chestnut tree.

"Then I'll manage four," cried a tall sycamore.

"Let's have five," said a chive.

"Hold it!" cried the other trees. "You're a herb, not a tree!"

"I know," said the chive, "but I rhyme with five."

And so it went on, right up to a date which took eight, a pine which took nine, and finally the world-record-breaker, a bamboo which took twenty-two.

At last, every one of the birds, animals and insects had found a new home, and the forest was able to settle down again. But no-one was happy about the nasty tree's behaviour. Such selfishness, they felt, should not be ignored, and so another conference was held in order to work out a suitable punishment.

How would *you* have punished the selfish tree? Perhaps you'd have taken away its fruit, stripped off its leaves, smacked its bottom, or sent it to bed without any supper. But the birds, animals and insects worked out an even better punishment, which all of them could help to impose.

You see, all birds, animals and insects have to eat and drink, just like us. And just like us, they have to get rid of the waste that they can't digest. They tend to let it out wherever they happen to be at the time, which is why you can be walking innocently along the road and suddenly find something soft and smelly sticking to your foot or – even worse – landing on your head.

The punishment to be given to the selfish tree was that in future all the waste matter would be left on it, over it, or under it. The selfish tree was to become the forest toilet.

Before long, the selfish tree had become the stinky tree, and every leaf, twig, branch and root was covered in dung. The birds took to dropping their waste matter from ever greater heights, while the animals and insects simply held their breath while they performed, and then scurried away as fast as their legs or wings could carry them.

As for the stinky tree itself, it would also have scurried away if it had had legs or wings to scurry with. But not only are trees unable to move, they're also unable to defend themselves, and so the coating of brown and

white became ever thicker, and the smell
became ever stinkier.

"Please . . . phew . . . please . . . ouf!" cried
the selfish tree. "No more . . . ugh . . . no
more . . . yuck! I'm sorry for what I did, and
I'll never be selfish again!"

It even promised to take all the birds and
animals and insects back again, but of course
none of them wanted to nest in a tree that
smelt worse than a gorilla's armpit, a sweaty
foot, and a cow's bottom all rolled into one.

There was one big problem with this
punishment, and it was a problem that soon
required an urgent solution. The smell from
the stinky tree didn't confine itself to the
stinky tree alone. It spread. And the longer
the punishment went on, the wider the effect
was felt. Eventually, the whole forest was
holding its nose and longing for the good old
days of stinklessness.

And although the stinky tree had
apologized, all the birds, animals and insects
had got into the habit of leaving their dung
there, and habits are very difficult things to
change. So the smell got worse, and worse,
and worse . . .

How was it made to go away? And why are there no stinky trees now? Well, it's all thanks to two insects, one of which was a fly, and one of which was a beetle. People often ask what use are flies and beetles, and the answer is that some flies and some beetles are simply brilliant when it comes to stink-removal. Do you know how they do it? If you want to know, read on.

The flies and the beetles lay their eggs in dung. Yes, they do. That may seem a funny place to lay eggs, but since you've never laid an egg yourself, how do you know which is a funny place and which is a normal place? Maybe the flies and the beetles reckon that nobody would fancy eating eggs laid in dung, and so their babies will be quite safe there. Would you like an egg covered in dung? Of course you wouldn't, so the flies and the beetles aren't stupid, are they?

When the eggs hatch into larvae, they eat the dung. Now *you* wouldn't want to eat dung, would you? But again that shows how clever the flies and beetles are, because they know that nobody else is going to take their food from them. So they can eat away to their hearts' content.

And that's how the problem of the stinky tree was solved. The flies and beetles went out and laid their eggs in the muck, then their larvae popped out of the eggs, and gobbled it all up. Each larva grew nice and fat, the muck soon disappeared, the smell disappeared with it, the birds, animals and insects made their nests in the tree again, and the tree was very happy to have them back.

It was some time before all the other birds, animals and insects got used to leaving their dung elsewhere in the forest, but the flies and beetles just went on laying their eggs there till the habit was broken. And now if you mention the stinky tree, nobody will know which tree you mean. The only trace that remains is the name given to the tree when the flies and beetles moved in, for even today we still talk of going to the larvatree.

My Brother is a Pig

Sharon Creech

My Brother is a Pig

Sharon Creech

I didn't mean to turn my brother into a pig, but I did, and it happened like this:

On Saturdays, my dad likes to clomp around car boot sales searching for treasures, and I like to go with him. My little brother Joey usually tags along too, but he is always a royal pain, whingeing on about how tired he is and how hungry and how hot or how cold.

You'd be amazed at what people practically

give away at these sales. They stuff their car boots with all sorts of things which they are more than happy to sell to complete strangers.

We always come home with something. This doesn't make my mother too pleased, because she thinks it is all junk, but she just doesn't use her imagination.

It was at one of these sales that I found the magic kit. It was tucked under a pile of old games and puzzles in a car boot. A gnarly old lady with a pointy nose and no teeth was bent over her treasures, taping little bitty price tags to things. Every now and then she'd stop and squeeze her hands together and roll them around each other as if she were rolling an invisible snowball.

I noticed the word MAGIC on the corner of a box and asked the gnarly old lady if I could look at it. She rolled her hands around and licked her lips. "Sure, my little one, sure you can." Her voice sounded as if it came out of the back of her nose.

Joey was tugging at my shirt. "I'm hungry, Claire, I'm *hungry*!"

"Let go," I said. "Let me just look at this magic kit, will you?"

"I'm *hungry*, Claire. I'm *cold*."

The magic kit box was dented and one corner chewed off, but the things inside looked as if they had never been used. There were two silk scarves, three plastic cups, a crystal, a rolled up tube of papery flowers, a magic wand, a booklet of magic spells, and three tiny bottles containing coloured liquids.

I bought it. As I walked away, the gnarly old woman said, "Heh, heh, heh. You be careful there. You be real careful."

"I'm *hungry*, Claire," Joey wailed. "I'm cold. I'm tired."

On the way home, Joey kept trying to grab my magic set.

"Get away," I said. "It's mine."

"Daaaaad," Joey wailed. "Dad, Claire won't let me look at the magic thingy."

"Let him see it," my dad said.

Joey dumped all the contents of the box onto the seat and got his sticky fingers all over everything. "I want this," he said, holding up one of the silk scarves and putting it on his head.

"Let go," I said. "It's mine. Put it back."

"Daaaad—"

It was like that all the way home. I tried to ignore him. I was leafing through the booklet of spells, but I couldn't concentrate with him dropping things on the floor and messing everything up. I noticed a couple of strange words in the book: *palulah* and *padiddle* and *padong*. *Padong* seemed pretty important because it was used a lot, and there was even a picture of a magician holding up the magic wand and saying, "*Padong!*" All sorts of fireworks were exploding out of his magic wand. It looked really good.

Crack! Joey had sat on one of the plastic cups.

"Look at what you've done," I said. "You nincompoop."

"Daaaad—" Joey cried.

Woosh! The yellow silk scarf on Joey's head blew out of the window.

"Hey – that's mine – it's gone – you triple nincompoop—"

"Daaaad—"

When we got home, I snatched the remains of my magic kit and ran upstairs. I was examining the magic wand when Joey came to the door.

"I want to do magic," he said. "I want to. *Now*."

"You'd better watch it," I warned. "Or I'll turn you into something dreadful."

"You will not."

"I will. I'll turn you into a-a-a pig! A slobbery, ugly, fat pig!"

"You will not."

"I will too." I waved the wand in the air. "*Palulah! Padiddle!*" I waved the wand around his head. "*Padong!*"

Fireworks spurted out of the wand and blue smoke filled the air and there was a tremendous popping and crunching sound and then – *Snort! Snort!*

I dropped the magic wand.

There at my feet was a big, hairy, fat, slobbery pig. It looked up at me with a puzzled expression. *Snort! Snort!*

My brother was a pig.

Snort! Snort! My pig brother shoved his fat snout at my legs. His pink and grey hooves trampled my feet. He started rooting around the room, pushing his snout into my clothes and my duvet, slobbering over everything in sight.

"Quit it," I said. "Turn back into Joey. Go away, pig."

The pig scrabbled under my bed and out the other side. It trotted all around the room, pushing and slobbering and making a terrible mess.

I picked up the wand. *"Padiddle-ulah."* *"Padoddle-paliddle."* I couldn't remember the words. Where was that booklet? I searched my desk, my bed, the floor.

The pig charged at me. It was carrying something in its mouth.

"Drop it," I said, pulling the torn, wet, slobber-covered booklet from the pig's mouth.

"Palulah! Padiddle!" I read as I waved the wand around the pig's head. *"Padong!"*

Fireworks burst into the air. Blue smoke swirled all around.

Snort! Snort! Snort! Snort!

Now there were *two* pigs. They chased each other around the room, knocking over my chair and my lamp. They pulled the duvet onto the floor and dragged it under the bed.

I dashed for the door and leaped into the hall, closing the door quickly behind me.

I had a feeling I was in deep, deep trouble.

167

I crept downstairs. "Dad?"

"Where's Joey?" he said. "Are you watching him?"

"He's upstairs."

"What's all that racket? It sounds like a herd of animals. Go and see what he's up to."

"Joey's a pig, Dad."

"Don't call your brother a pig."

"No, I mean he *really* is a pig. Two pigs, actually."

"Claire, that's enough of that. Don't talk that way about your brother."

"Will you *listen* to me?" I said. "He's big and fat and slobbery and—"

"Claire, you stop that this instant. Up to your room. *Now*! Not another word out of you."

Reluctantly, I crept back upstairs. There was a terrible snorting and crashing coming from my room. I peeked inside.

The room was a shambles: furniture toppled this way and that, the lamp broken, clothes strewn across the floor, papers chewed. The pigs were in the midst of chomping their way through my science book.

Maybe I should feed them. Maybe it would calm them down.

In the kitchen I grabbed the biggest bowl I could find. In it I dumped a box of cereal and a bottle of milk. It looked like the sort of slop a pig might eat. But it was not quite disgusting enough. What else did pigs eat? Maybe they ate worms.

Outside, I dug around the fence until I found three slimy worms. I chopped them up and added them to the cereal.

As I was sneaking back upstairs, my father appeared.

"Claire! Didn't I send you to your room?"

"I'm just going."

"What in the world have you got in that bowl?"

"Food," I said.

"Well, don't make a pig of yourself."

"I'll try very hard not to."

"And make Joey stop that racket up there."

"I'll try very hard," I said.

Upstairs, the pigs had finished my science book and were rooting around for something else. "Here piggies," I said. "Come and get some slop."

They buried their heads in the bowl, pushing and shoving and slurping. Cereal-worm-mash splattered everywhere. They cleaned out that bowl in five seconds flat and then they crawled under my bed, dragging the duvet with them, and fell asleep.

I grabbed the magic booklet and frantically leafed through it. Bits were missing.

There was a knock on the door, followed by Dad's head peering around it. "*What* in the world—?" He looked at the toppled furniture, the broken lamp, the trampled clothes. "This place looks like a pig sty!"

"Exactly," I agreed.
"Claire, get this cleaned up right now!"

"I think you should look under my bed," I said. I figured I'd better get it over with. He'd better see for himself.

"No thank you," he said coldly. "I've seen quite enough. You have exactly one hour to clean up this pig sty before your mother gets home." He slammed the door.

I didn't know what to do. I sat down on my bed. "I wish it was like it used to be," I said, skimming through the booklet. Then I saw these words: *"How to reverse a spell."*

Hurray! That was it. I read the directions. It said to dip the magic wand in each of the three bottles of coloured liquids: first into the red one, then the blue one, then the yellow one. Then, while the wand was still wet, wave it over the object and say the first two words in reverse order: first *padiddle*, then *palulah*. Wave the wand again and shout *Padong!* twice.

I found the three bottles of liquid, put them on my desk, opened them and dipped the wand in the red one, then the blue one, and lastly in the yellow one. I jumped on my bed. *"Padiddle! Palulah!"* I waved the wand again. *"Padong! Padong!"*

Tremendous fireworks spurted all around. The bottles of liquid toppled off the desk, spilling onto the carpet. Blue smoke whizzed around the room. I fell to the floor.

"Daaaad—"

And there in front of me was Joey, sitting on my duvet, his mouth covered with the cereal-worm slop. "Daaaad—" he wailed.

I was never so happy to see a slop-covered brother in all my life. I tried to hug him, but he ran out of the room. "Daaaad—" he cried.

You can imagine how relieved I was.

Now I have only one problem. Somehow, in reversing that last magic spell, I not only turned two pigs back into one Joey, but I turned my bed into a tree.

That's going to take some explaining.

Pigeon Talk

Vivien Alcock

Pigeon Talk

Vivien Alcock

The corner house was half hidden by low fruit trees and rickety fences. Hundreds of pigeons sat on the roof and on the branches of the apple trees, murmuring softly to one another.

"Cu-cu-*coo-oo*, cu-cu-*coo-oo*."

Jessie Brown loved to hear them. The children passed the house on their way to school. At least, her sister Alice and the

Hudson boys, Robert and Tim, passed it without a glance. But Jessie always stopped.

It made Alice cross.

"Don't lag behind!" she'd yell. "You're such a baby! Mum told me to look after you and how can I, if you're not there?"

"I only wanted to look at the pigeons," Jessie said.

Robert, a sturdy boy, with fat red cheeks, told her it was dangerous to stand there.

"Why?"

"Because the pigeons will splat on you," he said, sniggering. Alice told him not to be rude.

That night, when Jessie and her sister were in their room, getting ready for bed, Alice said, "You know that house with the pigeons, Jessie? Who do you think lives there?"

"I don't know." Jessie had never seen anyone come out of the faded blue door. When she'd peeped through the chinks in the fence, she'd never seen anyone in the garden. Only pigeons, pecking in the grass.

"Who lives there?" she asked.

"A wicked witch," Alice said.

Jessie sniffed. Her older sister had a face like an angel's but Jessie knew she often told lies. Like the time she'd told Jessie that Mr Hudson next door was a vampire who turned into a bat at night and slept hanging upside down from the light fitting.

"If he calls here, don't let him in," she'd said, "or he'll drink our blood."

So the next time Mr Hudson had called at their house to borrow some milk, Jessie had screamed and slammed the door in his face. It had been very difficult to explain this to her parents. One look at Alice's face had warned her not to mention vampires, so she'd said she'd mistaken him for a burglar. Dad had told her not to be so silly. "You've known Mr Hudson for years," he'd said. Alice had winked at her.

I'll never believe anything she tells me ever again, Jessie had thought.

Now, remembering this and other similar occassions, she said calmly, "Witches have cats, not pigeons."

"Ah," Alice said, "You don't know everything." She settled herself comfortably on the foot of Jessie's bed. "This witch did have a cat once called Perloma. But one day some bad children threw stones at it and chased it away and it never came back. In revenge, she

changed them all into pigeons. Haven't you
ever wondered why they never sit on any of
the other houses in Rimm Hill? Only on hers.
It's because they hope one day she'll relent
and change them back."

It couldn't be true and yet—Jessie had seen
the pigeons circling in the sky, and coming
back, always coming back to that one house.
The house with the apple trees and the blue
door. But she said stubbornly, "I don't believe
you. Witches turn people into frogs and toads.
Why does *she* turn them into pigeons?"

Alice leaned towards her and licked her lips.
"Because she likes pigeon pie," she whispered.
"She feeds them, she fattens them, then she
cooks them in a pie."

"I don't believe you," Jessie said again.

But that night she dreamed she was a
pigeon sitting on the roof of the house in Rimm
Hill. And all the other pigeons crowded round
her, murmuring mournfully.

"She'll cook you *too-ooo*, cook you *too-ooo*."

The next day was bright and hot. Jessie told
herself that dreams were only dreams and
Alice was a mean liar and there were no such
things as witches. But as they came towards

the house, she could hear the low purring of
the birds, and they still seemed to say,

"Cook you *too-oo*, cook you *too-oo*."

"No, you won't!" she muttered.

Tim Hudson looked at her. He was younger
than his brother, a small, quiet boy, timid as
a mouse. He never spoke to her, though he
sometimes smiled. Perhaps he was shy.
Perhaps the cat had got his tongue.

"Do you know who lives in this house, Tim?"
she asked.

"A wicked witch," he said, "that's what they
say. Do you believe in witches?"

179

"No. Do you?"

"No. No, I don't," he said, but he didn't sound too sure.

They had stopped and were looking over the gate towards the blue front door. Parked against the wall beside it was an old-fashioned broomstick, a bundle of twigs tied round the end of a pole.

"Look!" Jessie cried. "A witch's broomstick!"

As they stared at it, they heard the sound of a bolt being drawn, and the doorhandle began to turn.

"Quick!" Tim cried, and they fled after Alice and Robert who were some way ahead.

"Are you sure you don't believe in witches?" Jessie whispered to him when she'd recovered her breath.

"Are you sure *you* don't?" he retorted, and they smiled sheepishly at one another.

After that, they often walked together, lagging a little behind Alice and Robert. At first they hurried past the house with the pigeons but after a week or two they became bolder and would stop and stare. They never saw the witch, if a witch she was. They sometimes waved in case she was hiding behind her curtains but there was no answering wave. And the pigeons sat on the roof and in the trees, watching them and murmuring to one another.

"What do you think the pigeons are saying?" Jessie asked Tim.

"Pigeons can't talk," he told her, laughing. "They only know one word – Coo. It's hardly enough for a conversation."

A week later, on their way back from school, they saw the pigeons fluttering around the house in an odd, disorganised way. Alice and Robert didn't notice and walked on. But Jessie stopped, puzzled, for the birds were making odd unfamiliar noises. "What's the matter with them?" she said. "Has something frightened them?"

"A cat, I expect. Look out! Here they come!" Tim cried.

The pigeons were all around them now. They flew so close that the children could feel the wind of their wings fanning their cheeks, and see the frantic expressions in their small round eyes.

"They're trying to tell us something," Jessie said, "but I can't make it out."

"Perhaps they're hungry. Perhaps nobody's fed them today."

"Do you think the witch is dead?" Jessie asked.

"I don't know. She could be ill."

"I'd better go and see," Jessie said, for the pigeons were now flying into the garden and it seemed to her that they were calling her,

"C-come *too-oo*, you *too-oo*!"

"Jessie, wait! Supposing it's a trap?" Tim cried, but she was already through the gate and out of sight round the side of the house. He ran after her, shouting, "Jessie, come back! Come back!"

Robert and Alice, some way ahead, heard him and turned. "Where are the kids?" Alice demanded, suddenly frightened. "I can't see them. Where have they gone?"

Jessie and Tim were in the witch's garden. As they came through the apple trees, pigeons exploded from the ground. At first they could only see wings, pale feathers flying, dazzling their eyes. Then, as the birds settled in the trees, they saw a fat woman in a flowered dress lying in the middle of a small shaggy lawn.

"The witch!" Tim whispered.

She was not dead. They could hear her harsh snoring breath above the sound of the birds. She was lying on her back, her plump face oddly distorted, her eyes wide open and staring.

"Go next door and ask them to ring for an ambulance," Jessie said. "Tell them she's had a fit or something. Quick, Tim."

He ran off without arguing.

Jessie sat on the grass beside the old lady. Or the witch, if a witch she was. "You'll be all right," she told her, for the woman's eyes looked frightened. "The ambulance will be here in a minute. Don't worry."

The old lady seemed to be trying to say something but could only grunt. Her brown eyes turned sideways and then looked back at Jessie. Then sideways again and back.

"What is it?" Jessie asked.

The woman flapped her hand over, palm upwards on the grass. A pigeon hopped onto it, as if hoping for food. Jessie gently pushed it away.

"Are you worried about your pigeons?" she asked. "We'll look after them, if you like. We'll feed them for you, me and Tim." She felt the fingers tighten a little and then relax. The brown eyes looked happier.

Jessie sat in the peaceful garden, holding the old lady's hand, and listening to the sound of the pigeons talking. She heard quite clearly what they were saying.

Then everyone came running, scattering the birds into the sky. First it was Alice and Robert, then Tim and the next-door neighbour who told them the ambulance was on its way and wrapped a warm blanket round the old lady. Then the ambulance came singing down the road. The old lady was lifted gently onto a stretcher and carried out to where the ambulance waited, with its doors open.

"Is she your gran?" one of the paramedics asked Jessie.

"No," she said. "Me and Tim, we're her friends. We're going to feed her pigeons for her."

The man smiled and told her the old lady was going to be all right. "She's lucky to have such good friends," he said before he shut the door and the ambulance moved off.

Everyone was pleased with her and Tim.

Mum and Dad, when they heard about it, said they'd been splendid, noticing something was wrong and calling for help so quickly. Even Alice seemed impressed.

That night, she sat on the foot of Jessie's bed. "It was very brave of you to go into her garden, Jess, after I'd told you she was a witch. She isn't really, you know. I just made it up."

"I knew that. I knew she wasn't a witch."

"How? I've always fooled you before. How did you know it wasn't true this time?"

"I asked the pigeons and they told me," Jessie replied.

Sitting waiting for the ambulance, she had heard them saying over and over again,

"No, not *true-ooo, not true-ooo*, no!"

"Pigeons can't talk, Jess," Alice protested, but Jessie just laughed.

"You don't know everything," she said.

The Bear

Stephen Elboz

The Bear

Stephen Elboz

It's no fun being grounded, especially when it's not your fault. I mean, I admit I kicked the football: but how was I to know the wind would change and make it swing round like that? Anyway, I've always said it was a stupid place to put a greenhouse.

After Dad had stopped jumping up and down, he said, "Joe, why is it you always attract trouble? What you need is something

189

to keep you out of mischief." That was when Mum remembered the card in the newsagent's window. It seemed Mrs Pendergast, at the big house, wanted someone to keep her visiting grandson amused.

Dad's eyes positively lit up when he discovered she was prepared to pay and he telephoned with indecent haste so that everything was arranged.

That afternoon I found myself walking up to the big house. You had to go through these stone gates with an eagle on either side; behind them was a drive lined with trees. It was really long. Serves 'em right, I thought, if I fall down exhausted at the end. Mrs Pendergast would prob'ly have to give me my money and send me home again. Well, that cheered me up no end and I began to whistle.

Then I saw the house with Mrs Pendergast waiting on the steps and didn't whistle any more. She was frowning like a bulldog that had swallowed a wasp.

"You're late!" she boomed at me – like it was my fault her house was so far from the road.

"Come in," she said coldly, "and try not to touch anything."

Without another word I followed her into the hallway. Well, talk about grand. It had more pillars than a wedding cake. Then Mrs Pendergast went into a room where the furniture had golden tassels and in the cabinets were lots of china things my mum would have killed for. Perched on one of the sofas was this little blond kid.

"This is my grandson, Simon," announced Mrs Pendergast proudly.

I was shocked. The kid looked about six years old – nearly half my age! – with these large puppy dog eyes. Too late I realised the bitter truth. Dad had sold me into slavery as a *babysitter* to pay for his rotten greenhouse.

The kid climbed down off the sofa, came over and held out a pink mitt. He actually wanted me to shake hands!

"Pleased to meet you, Joe," he said – and do you know I think he really meant it.

"Splendid!" cooed ol' Mrs Pendergast. "Play nicely together and there'll be jelly and ice cream for tea."

I turned my look of injured pride on her, only to find she had already swept from the room.

"I'm glad you've arrived, Joe," the kid was saying. "Now we can start the bear hunt."

Bear hunt! I ask you. Was everyone here completely mad? I gazed at the kid pityingly and decided to let him down gently.

"As it happens, there are no bears in England," I informed him with all the authority of my age. "Least ways no bears you can hunt."

At this the kid got all excited – as if I'd taken his rattle away or something. "There are! There are!" he shouted, dancing about as though his feet were on fire and he was trying to stamp them out. "One sleeps on my bed every night and brings me my breakfast in the morning. He lives here with my grandma."

Coolly I fixed him eye to eye. "Oh yeah," I said. "Show me."

To give the kid credit he didn't back down. He just hared out into the hallway and up the stairs. At first I strolled casually after him, but thinking I might lose him, I began to run.

On the second landing I saw a door swing to.

Now I don't mind admitting that at this stage I was getting a tiny bit worried. The kid was so sure of himself and the house was certainly big enough for a bear. I mean it was not entirely impossible. Robert Griggs kept a snake in his bedroom for a whole month before his mum found it. Hesitantly I turned the door handle.

"Simon!" I hissed through the gap.

Catching my own reflection in a flaking dressing-table mirror I smiled with relief, seeing just an ordinary bedroom. Definitely not a bear's cage I decided. But where had the kid gone?

Something inside the wardrobe moved. I crept up, turned the brass latch and –

"RRRRRRRRRRRRR!"

A great, dark creature pounced on me. I was at the door, halfway out when I heard laughing.

Blood boiling mad I spun round. The kid was jumping up and down on the bed, his gran's dressing-gown slowly peeling off his shoulders and a fox fur sliding off his head. I felt pretty stupid, I can tell you. I mean he's just a kid and I'm years older than he is and have things like swimming certificates and a penknife with eight blades.

193

"That's . . . that's not funny, Simon," I said darkly. "It could have been dangerous. I mean, what if I had thought you were a real bear and gone and killed you?"

"Fo-oled you! Fo-oled you!" he chanted in his squeaky kid voice, all the time jumping up and down on the creaking bed. "You thought I was a be-ar!"

"For the last time," I said with forced patience, "there is no bear."

"He's hi-ding! He's hi-ding!"

"OK," I said. "I didn't want to tell you this, but I know somethin' far more fright'nin'

194

than some stupid ol' bear."

Suddenly interested, the kid slithered off the bed and stood before me, lost in the over-sized dressing-gown.

"Oh? What?"

My brain was desperately trying to come up with something horrible enough to shock a little kid out of his socks. Five minutes later we stood in the bathroom. I pointed.

"The toilet?" said the kid throwing me a quizzical look.

"Course it's a toilet," I spluttered. Then I made my voice all mysterious. "What grown-ups never tell little kids like you is, that down every toilet lurks the bug-eyed King of the Underworld, protected by his army of vampire crocodiles."

"Wow," mouthed the kid, immediately jumping at the bait.

"Yeah. If the bug-eyed King of the Underworld doesn't like you he waits 'til you're sitting on the toilet, then he sends one of his vampire crocodiles through the pipes to bite you on the bum."

Pretty good, huh? I was just congratulating myself on the tale when I noticed this smile slowly creep across the kid's face.

"Oh, but not here," he piped up confidently. "My bear would frighten off your vampire crocodile."

"But they have jaws like this . . . and teeth like this . . . and claws like this . . ." I cried, gesturing like an idiot.

"My bear's even bigger and stronger," said the kid unimpressed.

Well this meant war. I was determined to scare him now. I mean, it had become a point of honour.

"Right, you asked for it," I said. "I'm going to tell you something no little kid should know, 'cause it's too dang'rous . . ." And narrowing my eyes I said, "To call the bug-eyed King of the Underworld himself, you must turn on the taps hard, then flush the toilet and blink your eyes quickly three times . . . and then, as you watch, this green, slimy hand rises up out of the toilet . . . and it'll be *him*."

"Do it then," sneered the kid. "I wouldn't be scared. My bear will protect me."

By now I half believed my story myself. I yanked on the bath taps, flushed the toilet

196

and began blinking like some idiot in need of a pair of glasses.

The kid folded his arms, half amused by my antics. Slowly the filling cistern fizzled into silence, and nothing was happening.

"Told you so," said the kid triumphantly. "I told you your bug-eyed King of the Underworld is a scaredy cat."

But I wasn't listening. I had something else to worry about. The taps . . . they wouldn't turn off.

"Oh," said the kid all innocent like. "I should have warned you. If you turn the taps full on, they get stuck."

Worriedly I noticed that the water was rising faster than it could empty away. The kid jumped up and down clapping his hands in delight.

I thought his gran ought to be pleased by just how well I was keeping him amused. Perhaps she'd pay me double . . . only when I went to find her, I couldn't open the door.

"You shouldn't have locked it, Joe," I heard the kid whisper over my shoulder. "Last time the key got stuck, a man had to climb up a ladder to rescue me. That was fun." The kid sounded so cheerful I could have flushed him down the toilet, blond curls and all.

Was it my fault nothing in this ol' house worked prop'ly? I mean, it wasn't as if there were warning signs or anything. I rushed back and pulled on the taps as hard as I could, but the water still kept gushing out.

"If my bear was here he'd be strong enough to turn them off," said the kid.

"For once and for all there is no—" I straightened up so quickly that I cracked my head on some shelves. I mean, what a stupid place to put them.

Just before I staggered back and fell down, I had time to see the whole lot come away from the wall sending about a million bottles of expensive bubble bath smashing into the water. And, as I sat rubbing my head, wond'ring what kind of maniac needs so much bubble bath, I felt something splatter onto me. I didn't have to look to know the bath was overflowing.

The kid and me watched with horrified fascination. First the water dripped. Then it trickled. Then it cascaded over the bath's side.

The kid giggled. "This is fun, Joe," he said,

like I had deliberately planned it. "And just look at those lovely bubbles."

"Oh no," I groaned as the foam began to grow like something in a science fiction movie. For a moment the kid was overwhelmed by it. I dragged him free and he glared up at me like some angry dwarf with a white foam beard.

Just then a piercing scream told me that Mrs Pendergast had noticed the water dripping through her ceiling. She came battering on the door, blaming *me* for everything.

"What have you done to my poor, dear Simon, you wicked boy?" she bellowed.

Poor, dear Simon, I want it known, was happily splashing about in the now ankle deep water. I mean, I was only keeping him amused like I was supposed to do. She should have been pleased.

"You'll not get away with this!" threatened Mrs Pendergast storming off.

Soon me and the kid found ourselves pinned to the furthest wall by a crazy, quivering mass of suds. The kid remained remarkably cheerful about it.

"Don't worry," I whispered in a tough, big

brother kind of way to reassure him.

"Oh I'm not worried," he beamed. "My bear will rescue us."

"Listen – shud-up about your stupid bear," I said bitterly. "If I hear one more time about —" Suddenly my jaw went slack in disbelief. Behind all those trillions of bubbles a dark, menacing shape had appeared and was fighting to break through. It growled angrily as its foot plunged into the bath water.

"See," smiled the kid. "I told you my bear would come."

"That isn't a bear," I gasped.

"You mean . . . it's the bug-eyed King of the Underworld?"

"No . . . a million times worse than either of 'em."

Suddenly the figure clawed itself free of the bubbles.

The kid clutched me. My throat went dry. Hands were reaching out to grab me.

"But Dad," I cried. "It wasn't my fault!"

The Cowboy of Paradise Farm

Elizabeth Laird

The Cowboy of Paradise Farm

Elizabeth Laird

One bright morning at Paradise Farm, Stewart Harvey, the farmer's son, came crashing down the stairs and into the kitchen. He looked at the clock. Ten minutes to nine already! Quickly, he tipped some cornflakes into his bowl, sploshed some milk over them and began to cram them into his mouth.

"You'll choke," warned his mum.

Stewart picked up his lunchbox.

"So long, partners. I gotta get out of town," he said, and dashed towards the door.

"You'd better run through the field," his dad called after him, "but don't forget to shut the gate behind you."

Stewart raced across the farmyard and wriggled under the fence into the cows' field.

"Hi there, Myrtle," he sang out to his favourite cow.

Myrtle mooed softly. She was used to Stewart. Her sisters, Ivy, Dewdrop, Petunia, Betty and Bandy-legs mooed too. They always did what Myrtle did.

Pottingdean Primary School was right next to Paradise Farm, just beyond the hedge at the bottom of the cows' field.

Stewart bounded down towards the gate that led into the playground. The bell had stopped ringing, and the children were quickly disappearing through the double doors that led into the cloakroom.

Stewart reached the gate, unlatched it, darted through and let it clang shut behind him. He began to race across the playground, but then he hesitated. The gate sounded as if it had shut. It looked as if it was shut. It must be shut, he thought. He ran into the school, after all his friends.

The morning ticked peacefully by. Up at the farm, Mrs Harvey was feeding the hens. Down in Pottingdean School, Miss Hackett, the headteacher, was writing lists in her office. In Mr Speckle's class, Stewart and all his friends were making a wildlife mural.

But up in the cows' field, something unusual was happening. Myrtle had pushed her pink wet nose against the gate at the bottom of her field, and it had swung wide, wide open.

"Maroomph!" snorted Myrtle joyfully, for she was a cow that loved adventures. Briskly, she trotted into the playground of Pottingdean School, and Ivy, Dewdrop, Petunia, Betty and Bandy-legs all trotted after her.

Meanwhile, in Mr Speckle's class the wildlife mural was coming along beautifully. Acres of painted green paper lay drying on the tables, and everyone was drawing rabbits, voles, shrews, hares, crows, skylarks, kestrels, dandelions, clover, thistles, spiders and worms to stick on it.

Stewart was absent-mindedly drawing a prickly cactus instead of the rabbit he was supposed to be doing, when he looked up and saw Myrtle's face pressed against the window.

"Waah!" he yelled, not because he was scared of Myrtle, but because he was surprised.

Mr Speckle jumped, and his glasses, which he always wore balanced on the end of his nose, fell off.

"Stewart," he said crossly, "don't shriek like that!"

"But sir . . ." began Stewart.

"That's *enough*!" said Mr Speckle, and he bent down and started groping about on the floor, looking for his glasses.

By now, everyone except for Mr Speckle had seen the cow too, only by this time there was not one, but six. Myrtle, Ivy, Dewdrop, Petunia, Betty and Bandy-legs were all trotting past the window. Chaos broke out.

"Oh look, sir. Cows!"

"There's hundreds and hundreds of them."

"Bet they're going to attack the school."

"Bet they're going to attack Miss Hackett's office."

"Bet they're going to attack Miss Hackett."

Mr Speckle was still hunting for his glasses.

The girls were trying to be helpful.

"I think I trod on them just now, sir. I heard a kind of crunching noise."

"You can borrow mine if you like, sir."

"You might see better if you sort of screw your eyes up, like this, sir."

At last, Mr Speckle found his glasses. They were cracked. He stood up, extremely annoyed.

"Be quiet!" he barked. "Sit down!"

The class subsided.

"Now then," said Mr Speckle, putting his broken glasses into his pocket. "What on earth was all that about?"

Mohinder got in first.

"In the playground, sir," he said, pointing out of the window. "Look. Loads and loads of cows."

Mr Speckle swivelled his head round to look.

There was not a cow to be seen. Myrtle, Ivy, Dewdrop, Petunia, Betty and Bandy-legs had just trotted on round the corner of the school.

"What nonsense," said Mr Speckle. "Now settle down, everyone, and get on quietly with your work," but with a puzzled frown, he opened the door that led directly from the

209

classroom into the playground, and went outside.

Mr Speckle was too late. Myrtle had seen a pair of doors. They were all scratched and bashed, just like the doors leading into the friendly old milking parlour up at the farm, and she had butted them open and hurtled right in, followed, of course, by Ivy, Dewdrop, Petunia, Betty and Bandy-legs.

To their surprise, instead of being in their milking parlour, the cows found themselves in a corridor lined with pegs from which hung brightly coloured coats and bags.

They looked around for a moment, not knowing what to do. Petunia took a bite out of Linda Miles' shoebag. Dewdrop sniffed at Lucy Fairhead's lunchbox. Bandy-legs nibbled at Mohinder's coat and left a silvery stream of slobber down the sleeve.

But Myrtle was made of sterner stuff. She ignored the coats and the bags, and trotting down the corridor, barged straight into Mr Speckle's classroom, and Ivy, Dewdrop, Petunia, Betty and Bandy-legs barged in after her.

There was a moment of total silence while

everyone froze in horror. Then there was a riot.

Lucy Fairhead screamed. Mohinder sat down in the tray of paints. Linda Miles practically fainted.

Stewart shook his head in disbelief.

"Myrtle!" he said. "And Ivy, Dewdrop, Petunia, Betty and Bandy-legs! How on *earth* did you get in here?"

The deafening sound of Mr Speckle's class in hysterics made the cows panic. They started charging round the room. Petunia

211

knocked Mr Speckle's desk over. Betty sat down on the nature display. Bandy-legs licked the mural. Stewart slid quietly up to Myrtle.

"Myrtle!" he cooed softly into her ear. "It's me, Stewart! Come with me, back to your nice field. The others will all follow you, Myrt. Be a leader – now!"

But the commotion had terrified Myrtle. She didn't even notice Stewart. She wheeled round and plunged out of the room, back into the corridor, and, of course, Ivy, Dewdrop, Petunia, Betty and Bandy-legs all plunged out after her, with Stewart in pursuit.

Mr Speckle, who had peered round the playground but had found nothing there, decided that his class had tricked him, and, very cross indeed, he went back inside at the very moment that the door leading out into the corridor shut behind Stewart and the cows. He looked at his devastated classroom in disbelief.

"What on *earth*'s been going on in here!" he roared.

Everyone was making so much noise they didn't even hear him.

"I'm going to fetch Miss Hackett at once,"

said Mr Speckle, and he marched out into the corridor.

Sitting in her office, still making lists, Miss Hackett was puzzled. The school was filled with strange sounds. Clatterings were coming from the kitchen. Boomings and tinklings could be heard in the percussion cupboard. There were crashes and thuds in every single classroom, along with the wild din of a hundred children shouting. She opened the door of her room and went out to see what was going on.

She walked along the corridor and looked into the hall where the tables were supposed to be laid out for dinner. It was as if a hurricane had swept through it. Benches were overturned, cutlery lay in drifts on the floor, and of the dinner ladies there was no sign.

Mystified, Miss Hackett turned round. What was that, disappearing round the corner at the end of the corridor? It looked like a long tail with a black tuft on the end. It looked as if it belonged to a ... Miss Hackett shut her eyes for a moment and opened them again. The thing, whatever it was, had disappeared.

"I must get my eyes tested," she thought.

A strange smell was coming from the library. It was a warm, farmyard, earthy kind of smell, like the smell of ... Miss Hackett sniffed, and opened the library door.

There, on the carpet, was a huge blob of something brown and warm and moist. It steamed gently.

Miss Hackett bent over it and sniffed. Surely it wasn't a ... It couldn't be a ... Not right here, in Pottingdean School library!

Mr Speckle, finding Miss Hackett's office empty, had set off in search of her. He found her at last in the library. She was standing as if in a trance, looking down at the floor.

"Miss Hackett!" said Mr Speckle, waving his arms wildly, "my class has gone mad! Completely mad!"

Miss Hackett didn't answer. Mr Speckle stepped closer to her, and felt his foot squelch into something soft and mushy. He bent down to see what it was.

"I don't believe it!" he wailed. "I've trodden in a cowpat!"

Meanwhile the cows, who had been

exploring the staffroom and frightening the teachers into fits, were trotting back down the corridor towards Mr Speckle's classroom. They had had enough of this scary, noisy place and they wanted to go back to their nice quiet field. Myrtle, still in the lead, had calmed down and had noticed Stewart for the first time. He was tiptoeing along beside her, murmuring soothingly. "Come on, Myrtle! Good girl! Come home with me! You know you want to."

At that moment, Miss Hackett and Mr Speckle flung open the library door, and saw that the corridor was full of cows. They gasped in horror.

"Stewart!" roared Miss Hackett.

"Miss Hackett!" gasped Stewart.

"Moo!" bellowed Myrtle.

"Cows!" wailed Mr Speckle.

"Mr Speckle!" croaked Stewart.

They all stood and looked at each other.

"Stewart!" said Miss Hackett at last. "Where do all these cows come from?"

"They're Dad's," said Stewart. "The big one's Myrtle, and the others are called . . ."

"I don't want to know what their names are,"

hissed Miss Hackett. "What are they doing in Pottingdean School?"

"It's all right, Miss Hackett, I can explain everything," said Stewart, out of habit. Then he stopped. He couldn't explain anything. He had no idea what had happened. Suddenly, a nasty thought occurred to him. Perhaps on his way to school in the morning he hadn't shut the gate of the cows' field properly after all. He certainly didn't want to explain that. He shook his head. "Well no, actually, I'm afraid I can't explain," he said, "but don't worry. I'll get them out of here. Come on, Myrtle!"

To everyone's astonishment, Myrtle obediently dropped her head and mooing gently, she followed Stewart along the corridor, through the cloakroom, out of the double doors and into the playground, and Ivy, Dewdrop, Petunia, Betty and Bandy-legs trotted along after her.

Then, giving them friendly whacks on the rump, and with cries of "Yahoo!" and "Gid along there, sisters!" Stewart drove the cows across the playground and back into their nice quiet field. Very carefully, he shut the gate, then he sauntered back across the playground, waving his hand modestly to the entire school, who were watching him from every window and greeting his return with wild cheers.

You will be glad to know that this story had a happy ending, or rather, several happy endings. Myrtle, Ivy, Dewdrop, Petunia, Betty and Bandy-legs realised after all that home was best, and they never strayed out of their field again.

Mr Speckle didn't bother to get his glasses mended. He thought he'd wear contact lenses instead in future, to save the bother of having his glasses drop off the end of his nose.

Miss Hackett took early retirement. She decided that living in the country was too much of a strain, and she moved to a flat right in the middle of Manchester, where she was certain never to see a cow from one year's end to the next.

As for Stewart, when he grew up he went off to the Wild West and became a famous cowboy. And he never, ever, left a gate open again.

The Gift

Sharon Creech

The Gift

Sharon Creech

On my ninth birthday, when I opened my present from Gran, I could hardly believe my eyeballs.

I had saved her present for last because *usually* Gran gives me the most perfect gifts. Not expensive ones, but neat ones. I am her only grandson and she spoils me. Or at least she *used* to.

One year she gave me a chemistry set with

which I could bubble up all kinds of perfectly amazing and disgusting smelly things, and another year she gave me a magic kit from which I learned to snatch coins out of people's ears.

Gran's presents had always been the best, and always a surprise. You never knew what she would come up with. My parents wouldn't let me ask for specific things, anyway. They thought that was rude. They thought you should let the giver give whatever he or she wanted.

So I had no idea whatsoever what would be in that box from Gran. It was a smallish box, long and thin and flat, wrapped in plain blue paper and tied in white ribbon. It looked like the sort of box that a watch would come in: a special watch, an underwater watch that glows in the dark and has alarm bells and buzzers and tells the date. The sort of watch that if you fell off your bike and landed on your wrist, it wouldn't even break. The watch, I mean. Your wrist might break, but the watch wouldn't because it would be a super-indestructible, amazing, magnificent watch.

I slowly removed the paper. I could hardly

wait. It was going to be terrific. It was going to be unbelievable. I lifted the lid.

It wasn't terrific. But it *was* unbelievable. Unbelievably boring. Unbelievably stupid. Unbelievably the most awful, stupid, boring gift anyone had ever given me – ever – in my whole entire life.

It was a pencil.

You heard me right: a *pencil*. I turned the box upside down and shook it and examined it carefully, just in case there was a huge amount of money in there, or anything else – anything at all. Oh please, I thought, please let there be something else in this box so that I can look up at my Gran, who is sitting there watching me, and say thank you without letting her see that I am immensely and completely and totally disappointed to be unwrapping a stupid, boring pencil.

Poor old Gran, I was thinking. She has lost her poor old brains. What could she have been thinking of – giving me a *pencil*?

There was nothing else in the box. I turned the pencil around in my fingers. "Mm," I said, "what a nice pencil. What an interesting pencil. I can always use a pencil. A person can never have too many pencils, can they? A pencil is certainly a useful thing, isn't it? You can do so many different and interesting and useful things with it, can't you?"

I was lying.

I couldn't stop myself, though. On I went. "You can write with it and you can – you can, um, *draw* with it, yes, that's a good thing to do with a pencil, isn't it? Write and draw *too*. It's just amazing all the amazing and unbelievable things—"

My father interrupted me, thank goodness, or I would have been blathering on like that for a few years. "Let's have some cake," he said.

"Cake, yes! What a great idea!" I agreed.

For a while, I forgot about the pencil. To tell you the truth, I had put it back in its box and tossed it on my desk and soon it was buried under piles of magazines and school books and gum wrappers.

About a week later, when I had to write a report for school, I cleared off my desk, and that's when I found it again. I took it out of its box and examined it.

It was a seven-sided wooden pencil covered

in colourful printed paper: the sort of pencil
you might expect the Queen to write with. No,
on second thoughts, the Queen would probably
have a gold pencil or at least a silver one.

The design on the pencil was of many-
coloured leaves: red ones, blue ones, green
ones, and tiny gold ones that shimmered in
the light. One end of the pencil was sharpened
into a black point and at the other end was a
simple, pink rubber.

That's about it. At least it was sharp, and
since I had a report to write, I thought I might
as well use it. What the heck.

I wasn't too good at school things. Teachers
were always on at me about my messy
handwriting and my poor spelling and my
"jumbled" thoughts. So I didn't much look
forward to writing reports. This one was
supposed to be about a true experience. Wow!
There's a thrilling topic for you.

I figured I'd write about the time I
accidentally exploded a jar of pickles with my
chemistry set. I was in a hurry to write,
because if I finished all my homework by eight
o'clock I could watch television for an hour. I
dashed something off and didn't even bother

to re-read it. It was done. That was good enough for me. Time for television!

Three days later, the teacher handed back my report. Usually I didn't bother to read the comments in the margins. They always said the same things: "Watch your spelling!" "Poor handwriting!" "Can't read this?!" "Incomplete sentence!" On and on. At the end of the paper, the teacher usually wrote, "Try harder" or "Is this finished?"

As I stuffed this report in my binder, I noticed a word written in the margin: "Terrific!"

Maybe I got someone else's report back by mistake. I looked at the name at the top of the paper. It was my name alright. Rather neatly written, too, I noticed.

I glanced down the left side of the first page. The teacher had written: "Very good!" and "Nice handwriting!" and "I like this."

I checked the name at the top again. Still mine.

All over the paper were these amazing comments. At the end, the teacher had written: "Very well done. This is so true and honest!"

226

At home, I showed the report to my parents. Normally I don't show them anything unless they jump up and down and insist, because then they repeat the same things the teacher did: "You ought to try harder. Can't you write more neatly?" On and on.

When they read this report about the chemistry explosion, I noticed that they kept glancing back at the top of the first page, just as I had done, to be sure they were reading *my* paper.

"Well," my father said. "Well, well, well."

"Did *you* write this?" my mother said. "I mean, it's just so neat – and – *good*."

227

That night I had another written assignment: describe the life cycle of a frog. Another thrilling topic. As I sat there, trying to think how to begin, I noticed the pencil again. I turned it around in my hands. I sharpened it. I started to write.

The report was handed back the following week. "How creative!" the teacher had written. "How original!" and "Very neat!" and "Well done!"

I showed my parents.

"Well," my father said. "Well, well, well."

My mother looked at the name at the top. "*You* wrote this?"

But the next day, the teacher handed back another paper. It was one that I had written in class, in ink, and I had thought it was quite good.

It wasn't. In the margins, the teacher had written: "Sloppy handwriting" and "What does this mean?" and "Watch your spelling."

I didn't show that paper to my parents. I hid it in my desk.

I started to wonder about the pencil with its red and blue and green and gold leaves. I picked it up and turned it around in my fingers.

Could it be lucky? Was it magic? Did it have a brain of its own?

For the next month, I wrote absolutely everything with that pencil. Homework, classwork. Maths, Science, English. It was amazing. Teachers were falling all over themselves writing "Well done!" and "Good handwriting!" and "How true!" and "How creative!" On and on and on.

I kept that pencil with me at all times. I guarded it as if it were made of pure gold. If someone asked to borrow a pencil, I gave them one of my old yellow chewed ones. One time, the boy sitting next to me reached for my special pencil saying, "Let me use this a minute, okay?" and I snatched it back so fast he couldn't even blink. I reacted as if he'd tried to steal a hundred pounds from me. "What's your *problem*?" he said. I gave him one of my old yellow chewed pencils. "Nothing," I said. "Nothing."

I sharpened that pencil about five times a day. I wrote and wrote and wrote with it. It was definitely magic. It knew how to spell. It knew how to use big words. It had very neat handwriting.

I started getting worried when I noticed how short it was getting. Oh *no*, I thought. Oh *no*. What will I do when it's gone?

I had nightmares in which I'd be running through a forest looking for my pencil. I'd be sweating and screaming. "Where are you? Where are you?"

I tried to press lightly when I used it, hoping that the lead would not be used up so fast. I tried not to sharpen it until it was worn right down to the wood.

By now, only a few soiled and smudged leaves were left on the short stub of the pencil. But the pink rubber was still clean. I had never rubbed out a single word, that's how perfect the pencil was. That's how brilliant it was. It didn't make mistakes.

I started writing shorter papers. If a teacher asked for one page, I'd write half a page, figuring I could save my pencil that way. The teachers started writing things like, "Very good, but a bit short" and "Please write more."

In desperation, I called my Gran and asked her if she had another pencil like the one she had given me.

"Oh, did you like it then?" she asked.

"Like it? Of course I *like* it. It's the best, it's perfect, it's magic. But where did you get it? Where can I buy more?"

"Oh, you can't *buy* them," she said. Her grandmother had given her three of these pencils when Gran was my age. Gran had used one of them, just as I had. She had worn it down to a tiny stub. Then she had saved the other two. "One of them I gave to you," she said.

"And the other one?" I asked. "There's one more? Where is it? Can I have it? I *must* have it. I've *got* to have it."

The next day she brought me the last flowered pencil. It was in a box, wrapped in blue paper, with white ribbon. She didn't say anything. She just handed me the box, and gave me a funny look.

That night I examined my short, worn-out pencil. There was about two inches left. Maybe I could discover what made it special. Then maybe I could make my own, and I would never run out.

I took one of my old yellow chewed pencils and a knife, and slit the yellow pencil down one side. Inside was a thin piece of lead surrounded by wood. Then I took my worn-out pencil with its coloured-leaved paper. I slit it down one side. Inside it looked the same as the yellow one: a thin piece of lead surrounded by wood. I held the two pieces of lead side by side. They looked the same. They felt the same. They even smelled the same.

As I put the lead back inside the coloured-leaved pencil, my hands shook, and the lead broke. I slid the two pieces of lead in, end to end, and closed the wood around it. I taped the pencil round and round, but when I tried to write with it, the lead wobbled.

It wouldn't work.

That night my assignment was to write a story about generosity. I used an old yellow pencil. I wrote *very* slowly. I even checked the dictionary to be sure I was spelling correctly. When I needed to rub out words, which was a lot, I used the rubber on the end of my worn-out coloured-leaved pencil.

I wrote about my grandmother's gift: the magic pencil.

At the end of the story, I said that she had given me one more pencil, her last one. It was in a flat box, wrapped in blue paper with white ribbon. I said that I wouldn't use it. I would keep it. Maybe some day I would have a grandson and on his birthday, I would give it to him.

I haven't got that assignment back yet. I wonder how I did.

The Mysterious Meadow

Joan Aiken

The Mysterious
Meadow

Joan Aiken

Old Mrs Lazarus had died, aged ninety-four. For the last sixty years she had owned Fox Hill Farm, up above Highbury Village. Now her family had all come together – or most of them – to attend her funeral, to hear her Will read, and to learn what was to become of the property. Fox Hill Farm covered several hundred acres, over the slope of Highbury Hill, and any estate so close to London was now very valuable indeed.

"It's a wonder she hung on to it for so long," big fat Saul Wodge, one of the grandsons over from Chicago, was saying to his cousin Mark Briskitt, a professor from Manchester. Saul owned nine Fun Parks, scattered all over America, and was about to open a tenth.

"Granny Lazarus grew wonderful crops – parsley, basil, sunflower seeds. She and Uncle Tod were into organic farming long ago, before the rest of the country had even heard of it. They were selling to big hotels and supermarkets."

"No wonder she wanted to be buried under a tree."

"*Very* peculiar – not very nice at all!" said Petunia Wodge, Saul's wife. "Buried under a *tree*? What kind of interment is *that*, I ask you?"

The ceremony had taken place under a young beech tree, one of a narrow belt of beeches forming a windbreak between a ploughed field and a piece of rough downland pasture which stretched alongside Highbury Common.

Little Rickie Wodge, youngest son of the great-great-grandchildren, had already found blackberries scattered over the brambles bordering the Common, and his cheeks were stained purple.

"*Rickie!* Come back out of that! What ever have you found? You'll poison yourself!"

Rickie's mother Lara was in Chicago, nursing his six-week-old sister. Petunia, Rickie's grandmother, took off after him like a fury, but she wore shiny black shoes with three-inch heels and a tight lavender-coloured skirt; there was no possible way she could catch up with him as he bounded about, faster than a fire-cracker, fizzing with glee. Brought up in an apartment on the twenty-first floor, he had never seen so much grass in his life.

Forty grown-up children were discussing the Will. Sarah Lazarus had lived so long that her three sons and two daughters had died before her.

"*Two acres* to each grandchild! Of their own choice! How in the name of reason is that ever going to be sorted out? It will need half a dozen computers. And how are we going to find everybody?"

One of Sarah's sons, Luke, had moved to Buenos Aires and had six children. None of these had turned up at the funeral.

"It's going to take twenty years to settle the question of who owns every different bit," groaned Titus, the eldest son of Tod Lazarus. "And, in the meantime, here's the Department of Transport wanting to run a bypass road across the hill, and Moko Supermarkets anxious to build a Superstore . . ."

Furiously he stamped on a beech-nut which a nervous squirrel had dropped from a branch overhead. Golden leaves were beginning to flutter down from the beeches.

The September sun shone warmly on the descendants of Sarah Lazarus as they paced about indignantly, reading copies of their grandmother's Will.

"And what about this clause? Titania's Piece? Which field is that, anyway?"

"It's the strip of pasture-land beyond the beech trees," Mark Briskitt told his cousin Dinsie from Florida.

"What does Great-grandma mean when she says she is leaving it to the Travellers? Who are the Travellers, in mercy's name?"

"Travellers are gypsies. Egyptians, they used to be called. I think they have always used this piece as a camp-ground, right back to the Middle Ages. I can remember when I was a boy," said Mark, "and I used to come here for holidays, quite often there would be half-a-dozen horse-drawn wagons up there. Once an old lady called Mrs Lee told my fortune."

All of a sudden he looked wistful, remembering those days.

"She ever say you'd make a million?" big fat Saul Wodge asked with a guffaw.

"No ... She said I'd come to the brink and step back from it. I often wondered what she meant ..."

"But how could Great-grandma Lazarus leave Titania's Piece to the Travellers? Who are they? Do they have any legal rights?"

"Some of the local people round here say that piece of land always has belonged to them." Truda, the wife of Titus, a thin dark girl, spoke hesitatingly.

"How could they ever prove that?" snapped Petunia Wodge.

"It's said there's a boggle-patch on that bit of land."

"And what," demanded Cousin Kent Lazurus from Poughkeepsie, "what, pray, is a boggle-patch?"

"It's an area of land surface that actually lies in another dimension. Belongs to other powers, you might say. So if you tread on it, for instance, you disappear," explained Mark, who was a professor of mathematics.

"Is that so?" demanded Saul Wodge, laughing even more heartily. "So, I just have to hike across that patch of pasture a few times, and I'll vanish clean away? Say! That would be a really *great* idea for a Fun Park. Let's give it a try!"

He strode off through the belt of trees to the rough downland turf beyond, and began methodically pacing backwards and forwards across it.

"Hey, Mark! How *big* is this alleged bogey-patch – or whatever you call it?" he shouted.

"Only about as big as a dinner-plate," Tansy, Mark's wife told him. She glanced about for her eight-year-old daughter. "Tish! Run and find your cousin Rickie and bring him down to the farmhouse for tea. It's time we were on our way."

Slowly all the cousins and second-cousins and their wives and children began to trickle away, leaving the high warm hillside where fallen leaves lay on thin, fine grass.

Voices floated back in gusts on the afternoon breeze.

"Shame to break up the estate, really . . ."

"A highway *and* a supermarket though – we'd all be millionaires . . ."

"But where can the Travellers be found? Do they have a legal address? Do they have a *lawyer*?"

"Who is Titania when she's at home?"

The sun slipped round the side of the hill. Dusk was beginning to creep into corners, under blackberry bushes, between the high straight trunks of beech trees.

Tish Briskitt and her cousin Rickie had found a hollow tree and made themselves a house in it.

Cousin Saul Wodge, red-faced and spluttering with laughter, still paced pertinaciously back and forth across the strip of grassland.

"Hey, watch me, fellas! I've just about covered it all, now!"

Nobody was paying much attention to him any more, except the two children, watching from their tree-house, and Cousin Mark from Manchester.

Tish's mother Tansy called the children again.

"Tish! Rickie! Will you come along now!"

But Rickie was wilful and made off, giggling and shrieking, in the opposite direction, after his grandfather Saul.

"Grandpa! Wait for me!"

"I'll catch Rickie!" shouted Tish. "I'll collar him, Mum! You'll see!"

Off she darted after Rickie, her black plaits flying out behind her.

Then they all saw big fat Saul suddenly vanish, like a match-flame blown out, like a thin sheet of glass turned sideways on.

"*Hey, fellas!*" he was calling, but his voice died away faintly on the wind.

Rickie, scudding after him, vanished in exactly the same way, two seconds later.

"*Mark*! NO!" shouted Mark's wife, rigid with

horror, at the edge of the meadowland.

Mark, halfway across the grass in pursuit of his young cousin, pulled up and stood still.

So did his daughter Tish, just behind him.

"Dad!" she wailed. "Where's Rickie gone? Where is Uncle Saul?"

Husband, wife, daughter, looked at one another for a long, long minute, in complete silence. Then, still silent, taking hands, holding tight on to one another, they began to walk down to the farm, away from Titania's Piece.

The sun slipped behind the hill.